A DEADLY RUSE

A Deadly Ruse

Linda Lonsdorf

To order additional copies of this book, contact:
Xlibris Corporation
1-888-795-4274
www.Xlibris.com
Orders@Xlibris.com
129184

Dear Nan,

This is a story of crimes against our beloved elderly. It's about life changing experiences as well. Sometimes when we think an event is horrible, it turns out to be divine intervention and a blessing.

There are lessons here to think about. Enjoy!

Linda Lonsdorf

Other books by the author:

Family Threat

Evil Injustice

DEDICATION

To all of the law enforcement everywhere who put their lives on the line every day to protect the public and those who are elderly. Your work is dangerous and challenging, and we appreciate and respect what you do. A special thanks to Deputy Mike Walsh who watches over my mother and her home.

Greater love hath no man than this, that a man lay down his life for his friends.

ACKNOWLEDGMENTS

A special thanks goes to retired captain James Yocum of the Akron Police Department who has spent countless hours reviewing my plots to make sure that the police procedures are accurate. He has been a great supporter of my efforts as well as a special friend.

Captain Yocum introduced me to Lt. Chip Westfall (Akron's SWAT team). Lieutenant Westfall spent several hours taking me on a tour of the SWAT vehicle, explaining how the plot in this novel would be handled by SWAT so that I could be accurate and realistic. He did give me permission to take a few liberties with that.

Another special thanks goes to Tom Secrest who has designed interesting covers for my novels. Thanks for your creativity and excitement in these efforts. Who knew when you sat across from me in elementary school and doodled in class that you would become a talented graphic artist who would one day design three novels for me? I cherish your friendship as well.

Andy Pfaff, owner of Lyons Photography and another Coventry Comet and friend, spent a lot of time with me in his studio, making the session fun and trying to capture my essence. I bring him a challenge, I'm sure, but he's always up to the challenge. Thanks for what you do.

Another special thanks goes to my wonderful husband, Dr. Kevin Lonsdorf. He is a seasoned physician who has a lot of medical experience, including ER experience he acquired in his earlier days. His endless wealth of medical knowledge helps me constantly with my novels. Besides always being there, night or day, to answer my medical questions, he is a great encourager and supporter of my writing endeavors. He is the perfect example of a helpmate, and he is my best friend.

Thanks to my many neighbors and friends who encourage me too and wish to be in my novels. Some of you made it in this time, so enjoy! (Just remember, Bob Forwark, you wanted to be the bad guy!)

CHAPTER 1

9:00 o'clock in the morning

"Good morning. This is Dexter Rabone from Eastern Capitol Bank. I'm the security director for the bank, and I'm wondering if I'm speaking to Mrs. Mabel Bender?"

"Yes, I'm Mabel Bender. Is there a problem, Mr. Ra . . . ?"

"That's R-A-B-O-N-E, pronounced *Rabonee*. Well, as a matter of fact, Mrs. Bender, there is, and I was wondering if this is a good time to speak with you."

"Yes. Today is as good as any."

"First, let me say there is no problem with your bank account whatsoever. Your money is perfectly safe. However, we have had a problem with one of our bank tellers, and we have narrowed it down to one of two of them who work at the branch you deal with. We have been aware of the problem for several months, and now that we see what is happening, we need to set the bait so we can terminate and prosecute this individual. This teller is focusing on our most vulnerable customers—the elderly."

"Oh, my. We are often the victims, aren't we?"

"If I could very briefly and succinctly describe what is happening, we would certainly appreciate your help. When one of our elderly customers comes in to withdraw some money from his savings account, the teller is withdrawing the entire amount, closing the account, and giving the

---

customer what they have asked for. She then pockets the remainder. We believe she conceals the money at her station, and perhaps when some of the tellers go to lunch or step away, she pockets the money. It isn't until that customer returns to the bank to deposit or withdraw more money from his or her account that they discover the account has been closed and there is no balance."

"Well, how many times has this happened?" asked Mabel.

"We would rather keep that confidential, Mrs. Bender, but suffice it to say that if it happens to even one of our customers, it is one too many and we will find the guilty employee, prosecute, and rectify the problem to our customer."

"So where do I fit in to this scenario?" asked Mabel sincerely. She had already figured out what this bank investigator would be asking her to do.

"Well, we were hoping to set this employee up by having one of our loyal customers who is elderly to temporarily withdraw a large sum of money, leaving a small balance and with our hidden cameras, see which of the two employees is doing it.

"The larger amount of money would remain in your possession at all times and can be returned to the account probably within the same day—with no loss of interest to you whatsoever. By then, we would have proof of her impropriety, make the arrest, and spare other elderly people of this victimization."

"Well, couldn't this employee do this to anyone, not just the elderly?"

"Actually, she could, but we know she has chosen the elderly purposefully because they don't go to the bank very often, and if they do, they usually send their children to withdraw, and the children aren't as mindful of how much their parent or grandparent has in the bank. The problem isn't immediately discovered. By the time it is, the trail is much colder."

"So, what do you need me to do?" Mabel asked.

"I was wondering if you could come to the bank—perhaps today—and withdraw all but $100 from your account so that we could watch the teller and see what she does with your balance."

"I'm sorry, but I don't drive any longer."

Of course, Eddie Flatt, a.k.a. Dexter Rabone, already knew that from his weeks of surveillance of Mabel Bender. He also knew she had one son, but he visited her only on weekends, if she was lucky. He worked at GOJO, a factory job that made soap, in the daytime and, hopefully, would not be available to take her to the bank right then.

"Do you have a son or daughter who could drive you here?" asked Dexter, keeping his professional tone.

"No, my son works of a day. He couldn't take me until the weekend."

"No, that won't work. This particular teller doesn't work on the weekend due to a hardship in her family."

"Oh. That probably explains why the poor soul is doing what she's doing."

"Perhaps, but as kindhearted as you sound, Mrs. Bender, she is still stealing and breaking the law. We will seek prosecution."

"Yes, I understand. I certainly do."

"Well, now, I'm wondering perhaps if you would allow me to pick you up and bring you to the bank, Mrs. Bender. I couldn't go in with you, of course, because the teller would recognize me and might suspect she is being watched. What we could do is, after you withdraw your money, I would return you to your home. Therefore, the money wouldn't leave your sight. We suspect it will take her less than an hour to put your balance in her purse. We have hidden cameras set up to watch everything so we have proof that will hold up in court. She won't feel or sense anyone watching her. However, the bank manager will be in her office watching it all play out on her computer. As soon as the teller has completed the illegal transaction, the manager will call the police and have her arrested. She will then call me, and I will escort you back to the bank to deposit your money back into your account. The money will never leave your possession. Once we know how she is doing it, we will prosecute her for the other customers who became victims as well and demand retribution."

"Well, I guess nothing bad can really happen as long as I'm escorted by the security director of the bank."

Eddie Flatt laughed impishly. "Yes, you're right there, Mrs. Bender. I guarantee the best protection for you and your money. In fact, the bank is willing to give you an added $100 for your inconvenience and possibly a further reward if the teller is prosecuted. Without help from one of our customers, we couldn't stop the crime."

"You say this will only take about an hour?"

"I would say no more than an hour or hour and a half as we will have you go in near the lunch hour."

"Well, if you're willing to come get me and will stay with me while I'm in possession of all that money, then I guess it will be all right."

"I promise not to leave your side, Mrs. Bender. By the way, I'm not sure how much money you have in your account as we keep the records confidential, but it doesn't really matter provided you leave a balance in of $100. That assures us of a prosecution."

"Well, what if she asks me why I'm taking so much out of my account?"

"Well, you don't have to tell her. It's none of her business. After all, it is your money and you have a right to reclaim it any time you so wish. Now, if you so wish, depending on how much you are withdrawing, you could make up a story that is logical to satisfy her. How much might we be talking about, Mrs. Bender?"

"I would be taking out approximately $50,000."

"Well, then, it's probably a very good idea that I will be escorting you home and back to the bank with that amount. So if she asked what your intentions were with that money and you were so inclined, you could tell her that you were withdrawing that money to give to your granddaughter who was getting married in the near future. You wanted to help pay for the wedding of her dreams or give her part of a down payment on a condo or something. I wouldn't get too elaborate on your story."

"Yes, that might work. Well, let's do it, Mr. Rabone."

"Thanks for being such a gutsy lady, Mrs. Bender. Let's hope our mission today succeeds. When I come to your door to pick you up, just so that you know who I am, I will be wearing a dark navy blue suit and will show you my bank badge with my title."

"And what time should I expect you?" Mabel asked.

"Would eleven o'clock be all right?"

"That would be fine, Mr. Rabone."

"One more thing, Mrs. Bender."

"What is that, Mr. Rabone?"

"Because of the delicacy of this problem and the bank's embarrassment that this could even happen at our bank, we would prefer you not to tell anyone about this. Our reputation is at stake. We take great pride in our bank, and we don't want one bad egg destroying the integrity of Eastern Capitol. And we certainly don't want our ruse to be foiled."

"Of course not," Mabel replied. "I will be ready at eleven o'clock."

CHAPTER 2

Eddie Flatt had rehearsed this conversation for many months, trying hard to sound professional and believable. He had his spiel perfected and had gotten lucrative results. Over a year had passed when he and his boyhood friend, Bobby Forwark, had mapped out this elaborate plan to scam the elderly of their hard-earned money. After all, they were the only ones who would fall for such a plan.

Eddie and Bobby had gone to Goodwill and purchased a very nice man's suit for $6 that fit Eddie perfectly. They had also purchased a very attractive man's attaché case that fit the part of an important banker. Then they made their way to Staples on S. Arlington Road and purchased a bag of name badges. Eddie was the smoother talker of the two, but Bobby had some knowledge about computers, so he typed the name of Dexter Rabone in black, bold print, and below it, his fake title, Security Director, Eastern Capitol Bank. It looked quite professional. If Eddie could just maintain his poise and act professional for several hours and not slip up, they could become the new owners of someone's lifetime savings.

If these people were stupid enough to buy in to such a crazy story, they didn't deserve to keep their money. What's the saying . . . *A fool and his money are soon parted*? Besides, what good was money just sitting around in a bank safe? Money was meant to be spent and enjoyed, and Eddie and Bobby had already proved they knew how to enjoy money to the fullest!

They grew up three houses down from each other. They rode the same school bus to school their entire lives. They were in many of the same classes together. They were inseparable at recess, lunch, and after school. They took turns playing tackle football in their backyards. They were truly connected in so many ways. Both of their parents were divorced; both of them struggled in school academically, and neither came from a caring, stable family. They suffered few rules or restrictions growing up, and neither had a sense of discipline or self-control.

Upon graduation, both tried to join the Air Force, and both were declined. Both had failed the ASVAB test, and both used enough drugs to fail the urine test. Now they had to redirect their lives. They actually graduated with no job skills, no accomplishments to impress on a résumé, no clearly defined goals, and no people skills. However, they were determined to get *rich*! That was a must. Their parents had failed them, the schools had failed them, and so they had to depend upon themselves to be innovative and find a way to live the good life. They finally put their heads together and found a way. It would require them to be refined, but for only short periods of time. Each had their own role, using their specific gifts for the cause, and however much money they were able to collect, they split.

This new adventure required some traveling, but here they were back in their old hometown. After they completed their mission here, they would have to leave town quickly and lie low for a while. So far each job had been pulled off successfully and without a paper trail to implicate them. Bonnie and Clyde should have been that lucky!

CHAPTER 3

11:00 o'clock in the morning

Dexter Rabone pulled up in the driveway of Mrs. Bender's home in the Kenmore area. He looked around to see if neighbors were walking the sidewalk, looking out their windows, or were even in sight. He saw no one, so that was good. He walked up to her door, and before he could knock, Mabel opened the door. She had a dress on and her purse in hand.

Dexter had his identification badge on his lapel in open view, identified himself to Mabel, and they walked to Dexter's rented silver 2010 Elantra.

"Good morning, Mrs. Bender. Again we appreciate your assistance with this problem. We do everything in our power to see that our elderly customers don't become victimized, and when we learn that it's happening from one of our own, we simply won't tolerate it. We will find them and prosecute to the fullest!" said Mr. Rabone with urgency and confidence.

"That's good to hear, Mr. Rabone."

"That's Mr. Rabone-e, Mrs. Bender. It's spelled with only one *e*, but it's pronounced as if it had two or ended with an *ey*."

"Oh, yes. I'm sorry. I forgot."

"No problem. Do you have your savings booklet with you?"

"Yes, I do."

"Good. Now, remember, you don't have to give the teller a reason, but if you do, make sure it's believable. Don't tarry in the bank or try to stare at the teller too long to make her curious or suspicious of you."

"No, I won't do that."

Bobby Forwark had entered the bank ten minutes before Eddie was to arrive there with Mrs. Bender. He saw two female tellers working behind the counter. He walked up to the redhead and asked if she could give him change for a fifty dollar bill. He noticed she was wearing a royal blue blouse with a black jacket over it and bright red lipstick. The name card at her station said Angie. The other teller was wearing a white blouse with a colorful neck scarf and only lip gloss. After he got the change, he left quickly, making sure that upon entry and exit of the bank, he was not in a good view of the bank cameras. He also was wearing a baseball cap with the visor extending far over his face to block a good, clear view of him.

As soon as he got to his car, he pulled away and went down the street to call Eddie on his cell phone.

Eddie answered immediately. He said nothing but just listened.

"Tell her to go to the teller with the bright blue blouse and black jacket, not the one with the white blouse."

To make things appear professional, even after Bobby had hung up, Eddie said, "Thanks, Mr. Secrest. I'll take care of that as soon as I get back to my office. The police report for that case is in a folder on the right corner of my desk for your review. I should be back to the office in another hour, hopefully." With that, he winked at Mrs. Bender and hung the phone up.

"Mrs. Bender, when you go in, make sure you step in the line of the teller wearing a bright blue blouse and a black jacket. Her name is Angie—there will be a name card by her station."

"Angie? I don't think I know which one she is."

Eddie was almost relieved to hear that. Of course, that is if the old lady wasn't forgetful.

"Well, no matter. Try not to engage in any more of a conversation as you need to with her."

"I would hate to think that the tellers I know would do something like that to me. Whoever it is must be pretty desperate."

Mr. Rabone explained to her that he would be waiting outside the bank to escort her home safely.

"Gotcha, Mr. Rabone. This shouldn't take long."

Eddie was sure hoping it wouldn't. He made sure that he parked on the side of the bank where the brick building had no windows and was not being used by customers. Whatever happened in the next few minutes would either be a good thing for Eddie Flatt or a bad thing. There were risks, but the way he and Bobby saw it, the risks were exceedingly minimal. They had been pulling this ruse for over two years. Actually, it had been four times over the years and in four different locations. That's what they had accounted for their success. Perhaps they shouldn't have come back to their hometown to pull this one, but it seemed like it was as good as any. They had a few more ruses to go before they planned to leave good old Akron for a life on a Caribbean beach.

CHAPTER 4

Mabel stepped out of the car, and with her passbook in one hand and her oversized black purse in the other, she stepped inside Eastern Capitol Bank. Immediately she saw the teller with the royal blue blouse and black jacket and saw the name tag, Angie, by her station. She didn't recognize this particular teller. In some ways, she was glad. She would have felt even more terrible to send someone she had had a relationship with away to prison. This young lady, however, looked so sweet. It was hard to fathom Angie could swindle someone out of his hard-earned money. However, Mr. Rabone could be wrong. Perhaps it's another one of the bank tellers.

"Good morning, young lady. I've come to withdraw some money out of my account," she said as she handed the teller her passbook.

"Okay. How much would you like to withdraw?" asked Angie.

"Fifty thousand dollars," said Mabel matter-of-factly.

"Fifty thousand dollars?" asked Angie without trying to seem surprised.

"Yes, ma'am."

"That would leave a balance of only a $100 in your account, Mrs. Bender."

"Yes, I believe that's correct."

"I'm not so sure we have that much money in our bank today. I will need to go get my manager."

And with that, Angie stepped away from her station and walked from behind the counter to a lady sitting in a private office. Mabel assumed she was the manager. The woman looked up. Mabel could see they were exchanging a conversation about her request and then the manager escorted Angie back to her station.

"So, Mrs. Bender, I understand you want to withdraw $50,000 from your account today?"

"Yes, ma'am."

"Would you want us to write you a certified check or make it out to a specific person?"

"No, I would like to have it in cash—hundreds or twenties would be preferred, please."

"We usually don't have that much money sitting here in the bank, but today we did get a shipment in from the Brinks truck. I think we might be able to do this for you today. Usually we need to know about a withdrawal of this size several days in advance so that we can make sure we have that large amount of cash in our bank.

"May we ask why you want to take so much out of your account? I mean, is everything okay, Mrs. Bender?"

"Yes, dear. My only granddaughter is engaged to be married, and I want to provide her the beautiful wedding she has always dreamed of."

"When is the wedding?"

"In the next few months. Now I really must get going as I have a busy afternoon, dear."

"Certainly, Mrs. Bender. We'll need to bring the money from the vault. It will take just a few minutes."

Mabel saw the two women whisper to each other and then they turned to go into another area of the bank where the vault most likely was. Only Angie returned, carrying a large, heavy sack.

Fortunately, the bank started getting very busy, and the other tellers were engaged with other customers. Angie counted the packs of money to Mrs. Bender, so she could count along and know she was getting the amount requested.

"We really don't recommend that you withdraw that much money out at once, Mrs. Bender. In fact, we usually don't even have that much money on hand at our bank. You just got lucky that we had a shipment arrive this morning. Please be very careful as you leave here."

"I will, dear. How sweet of you to care about that. I will be just fine. You be careful as well. Working in a bank could be a dangerous place too." Mabel looked Angie straight in the eyes and smiled sweetly and sincerely.

Angie thought her words were a little ominous and perhaps a wee bit strange, but the white-haired lady seemed very sweet. *She must be one terrific grandmother,* thought Angie, as she watched Mrs. Bender leave the bank and turn around the corner.

The next customer stepped up to her station so that Angie had no more time to focus on Mrs. Bender. It was business as usual.

CHAPTER 5

Mabel got in the car, and Rabone drove quickly out of the parking lot.

"So how did it go?" asked Eddie.

"Well, they asked me why I was withdrawing so much money, and Angie went and got the manager to oversee things. I thought they weren't going to give the money to me at first."

"That's pretty standard procedure. But they did give it to you, didn't they?" Eddie asked without looking too rambunctious.

"Oh, yes. They gave it to me. Angie seemed so genuinely sweet. I surely hope she isn't the thief."

"I know how you must feel, Mrs. Bender, but we know considerable money has been taken, and we have it narrowed down to Angie or one other teller. It's always disappointing when someone you put your trust in lets you down."

"Hmmmph!" responded Mabel as she sat pondering all of that.

As they pulled in to her driveway, Mabel asked Mr. Rabone if he might help her carry the money in as it was so heavy. He agreed while acting chivalrous.

Once they stepped inside the house, Mr. Rabone assured her it would only be a short time, and the bank would be calling him.

"Would you care for a hot cup of tea, Mr. Rabone, or perhaps a cold drink?"

"No thanks, Mrs. Bender. That's very kind of you. I will just have a seat here on your couch, if you don't mind, and quietly wait. Perhaps

I will open up my attaché case and get some work done on my laptop computer."

Eddie watched Mabel closely as she set down her oversized purse filled with the money along with another bag the bank provided for containing the large amount of currency.

"Were they able to give you the money in all twenties?" asked Mr. Rabone.

"No, they gave me some in packs of $100 bills also."

Mabel then opened up her purse and pulled out one of the packs to show Mr. Rabone.

"Well, it will be easier for the teller to count the money when you go to return it to your account."

"Right."

Once Eddie realized the mission had been successfully accomplished, he had no intentions of playing the game any further or allowing any human interference. Mabel had sat down in her comfy chair directly across from Eddie. He was sitting on the sofa with his attaché case on the floor by his feet. He put the attaché case on his lap and opened it up. He reached in and pulled out his .38 special, pointing it directly at Mabel's chest.

She looked surprised.

"So what's going on, Mr. Rabone? Or is your name Mr. Raboney as in full of bologna or Mr. Phoney?"

"Either of those would work, Mabel, dear. I'm sorry to have to do this. You were such an easy target."

"How about if I give you all of my money, you leave, and I keep my life?"

"That won't work, Mrs. B., because you would turn me in, and you could describe me."

"Son, do you realize that you could earn your money in an honest way and be so much happier?"

"Not true, Grandma. I'm really sorry, but I need to get on my way."

"Please, young man, I beg of you—"

With that, he pointed the gun at Mabel as she started to get up out of her chair and run. He hit her twice in the chest, and she fell back in her chair.

Eddie put the gun back in his attaché case. He found a dish towel in the kitchen and wiped off the doorknobs. He grabbed the money from her purse, snatched the bag of money, and quickly went out the side door, careful not to touch a thing. He started his car up, making sure no one was in sight. From the best he could tell, he had just pulled off a successful heist, but there would be a lot more Mabels to trick and a heck of a lot more money yet to inherit!

CHAPTER 6

Doug Conrad was sitting in his office reviewing a case when his phone rang. He looked up at his phone to see Caller ID and recognized the phone number as that of Paul. Paul was his oldest child, a senior at Ohio State University studying biology. He was always excited to talk to Paul and especially after their recent ordeal that led to the murder of Cynthia, Paul's mother. Quinton Reed, the murderer, had attempted to not only kill Doug's wife but his children as well. He almost succeeded except for the fact that during the attack, Paul was able to grab a bat and get the upper hand as he and Quinton struggled. Paul nearly beat him to death with the bat out of anger and fear. Later, Reed was convicted of killing Cynthia and sentenced to death. However, Reed managed to escape but was actually shot and killed by Donna Gifford, his newly hired employee who was at Conrad's house to help guard the house from another possible visit by Reed. In that incident, both Doug and his daughter Taylor were nearly killed by Reed. If it had not been for Donna Gifford's acute shooting ability, both very well could have died that night.

The horror was finally over, but Doug and his two kids were still feeling the paranoia and insecurities that come from such a tragedy. Both Paul and Taylor had gone through counseling. Because they had been so grounded in their faith, the counselor felt they were ready to move on after several months of counseling.

"Hi, Paul. Glad you called, son."

"Hi, Dad."

"How's school going?" asked Doug.

"Made the dean's list again, Dad."

"That's great, son. I wouldn't have been shocked if your grades had slipped some, given all what you've been through."

"Actually, I've buried myself in my studies, Dad, and stayed focused to avoid thinking about it. There's been a lot of lab work, so it's easy to get entrenched in the experiments."

"Well, make sure you have time to enjoy campus life too, and have a social life. You probably need some comic relief!"

"Actually, Dad, since our story has been printed in the papers and plastered on the news, I've become a chick magnet. The girls think I'm some kind of a hero, and they're asking me out. It's kind of crazy!"

"Well, I don't know if that's good or bad, son. Just be careful with that. You are certainly a hero and have earned admiration, but make sure the girls aren't just in love with heroes. You want them to see you as a whole package, not just one element."

"I'm good, Dad. Don't worry."

"Find a woman like your mom, and you'll have a winner, son."

"I know, Dad. I'm lookin'."

CHAPTER 7

Doug Conrad stepped into Donna Gifford's cubicle. Barnabus Johnson, his other newly hired employee, was apparently out of the office working on a case, so he felt he could have a private moment with Donna.

"Are you busy right now?"

"Not too busy to talk to my boss," she said with a smile on her face.

Doug also smiled rather sheepishly. While he was the sole owner of Conrad Confidential, he really never viewed his company as having a pecking order. He always viewed his company as a working, cooperative team.

"It's taken me awhile to process everything that happened the fateful night Quinton Reed came to my home to kill me—and nearly killed Taylor and me. I—"

"Doug, I can certainly appreciate your feelings. You don't need to—"

"Yes, I do. I mean I want to . . . We had so many people there that night to help protect us—risking their lives—I am still overwhelmed by it all. So many things could have gone wrong, and almost did . . . Had you not been upstairs in that room and so alert, things could have turned out differently. You had the skill and the acuity to see what was happening. Once I found out you were the shooter and put an end to our ongoing saga with Reed once and for all, I know I thanked you, but if you don't mind, or if you'd allow me, I would love to take you out for dinner. It's not a date—so don't misunderstand my intentions, but I want to show my gratitude to you, and I thought maybe since you are widowed as well, we could just have a relaxing dinner."

"That's very nice, Doug. I haven't really been out with anyone—not even a male family friend since Peter died. I needed time to adjust and to calm down. Under these circumstances, I accept your invitation to dinner, but you don't have to do this. I was doing my job, and I was glad I could be there—be at the right place at the right time. It was good to see my training pay off and there be a happy ending for a change."

"It was a happy ending for me and for my family, but for Ramona Reed and her three sons, I'm sure it gave them sad closure. He paused for a brief moment as though he were empathizing with that family's pain.

"Well, then. Since you accepted, how would this Saturday evening be at 6:30 p.m.? I will make reservations for Hyde Park Grille and will pick you up at 6:00 p.m.?"

"I'll be ready, Doug. You'll get to meet my mom, and of course, there is Blaze and be forewarned, Chunx."

"Chunx?"

"Yes, just be prepared."

"Okay."

Doug didn't know who or what Chunx was, but somehow he thought he might be in for a surprise.

Donna smiled impishly. She knew Chunx would draw out Doug's personality and give her further insight into this seemingly very nice man.

CHAPTER 8

Bobby Forwark had been perusing neighborhoods for weeks, seeking out elderly people who lived by themselves and had little or no company. Some of them went to their paper boxes or mailboxes walking with canes or struggling physically, bent over. Clearly they were frail. They all seemed oblivious to their surroundings. Their main focus was walking to the curb for their newspaper or mail and returning to their house without falling. He would write down their addresses and learn their names. He and Eddie would then discuss which of their ruses would work for that particular victim. Usually the old men wanted outside jobs done—roof repairs, awnings, shrubs trimmed, spoutings cleaned out, yard work, whereas many of the women needed things inside the home fixed such as leaky faucets or needed the furnace or fireplace checked. Women could easily be scared into paying for a damaged roof, however, so after a pretty hard storm, Bobby and Eddie would begin the scams.

Eddie was the smooth talker, and Bobby was more plebeian in behavior, presenting traits he couldn't change. He used poor grammar and didn't know differently. He nearly failed English and grammar every year he was in high school and barely graduated by the skin of his teeth. He bore a bourgeois appearance. So, actually, they complemented each other for pulling off a variety of ruses.

CHAPTER 9

Dan Bender was in his fifties. He had worked at GOJO Industries since 1987. His had been a factory job, but he had made a decent living over the years. He had led a rather simple life. He married fairly late in life and had no children.

His mother was widowed, and he made a point of visiting her at least once a week, usually on the weekend. When he was a child, his mother was persnickety about cleanliness. One of his most significant memories was of his mother checking his hands, his face, and behind his ears before he sat down to dinner. So he made sure his mom had a convenient size of Purell in every purse and one in every room in her house. He was an only child, but he was one of the few he ever knew who wasn't spoiled. He was very close to his mother and had the greatest respect for her. He tried to call her at least twice a week and touch base with her. She didn't drive, so if she needed something from the grocery store, he would see that she had it by the weekend. If it was an emergency, he made a special trip to obtain it for her and drop it off, even though they lived about twelve miles apart.

It was about 10:30 a.m. when Dan pulled into the driveway of his mother's home in Kenmore. He had called his mother to say he was leaving his house to come over, but she didn't answer the phone. He assumed she had stepped out to get the newspaper or was taking a shower and hadn't heard the phone ring. No matter. She always knew he came over every Saturday morning to take her to the grocery store and run any errands she might need. He had a key and could let himself in if need be.

He climbed the front porch stairs and banged on the front door. His mother was a little hard of hearing, so he rang the doorbell as well. He gazed around the neighborhood at the neighbor's house. Not much had changed since he had left the house where he had grown up. Everyone kept their yards up nice and seemed to watch out for each other. Most of the neighbors were elderly like his mother. All the kids had grown up and moved away.

He knocked once again and then peaked through the narrow window in the door. He wasn't able to see any activity. He decided to unlock the door and just go on in. He would call out her name as soon as he stepped in so as not to scare her.

"Hi, Mom. It's me. I'm coming in."

Usually she would call out his name and say hello, but there was nothing. That was so unusual he began to sense that something was wrong. When he stepped into the living room, he saw his mother slumped over in her chair. He thought at first that she was sleeping, but then he saw something dark on the front of her housedress. He called out her name.

"Mom. Mom?"

As soon as he touched her, he knew she was dead. Her arm was very cold. Then he saw that the stain on her dress was dark, dry blood. She had been dead for some time. He was confused. Had she hemorrhaged or something? What had happened? His heart was pounding, but he stepped to the phone and dialed 911.

"Your emergency, please."

"Yes, I just came inside my mom's house and found her dead. She's elderly, but I don't know what's happened."

"Your name, sir?"

"Dan. Dan Bender. My mom's name is Mabel Bender. She's seventy-eight years old."

"Are you calling from her residence, sir?"

"Yes."

"Would you verify the address, please. Our paramedics are on their way as are the police."

"Yes. Thank you. She lives at . . ."

He couldn't believe this was happening. She had been doing quite well. There really hadn't been much significantly wrong with his mother. She suffered from arthritis and had shingles once. She had macular degeneration but was still able to see okay. Otherwise, she had been doing quite well. He sat his mother up in the chair more, and then to his utter shock, he saw it—a bullet hole in her chest.

Anger, fear, and distress hit him all at once. Who would have done this to his mother? Why? Things like this happened to other people, not to people like her. As tears streamed down his cheeks, he heard the sirens come.

CHAPTER 10

Doug Conrad took a long, hard look at himself in the mirror. He hadn't done that for years. If he had a piece of lint on his shoulder or a stain of some sort before leaving the house, Cynthia would see it and call it to his attention. He wanted to make sure that he looked presentable. He felt nervous, but he didn't know why. After all, this wasn't a date. He was taking Donna Gifford to dinner in appreciation for killing Quinton Reed, a man who had sought for months to kill him and his family. He had succeeded in killing Cynthia and almost killed his daughter Taylor and himself. Had it not been for Donna. Donna Gifford. Reed had been given the death penalty and was even on his way to death row when he escaped and made a final attempt to destroy the Conrad family. The police and the SWAT team had even surrounded his home to protect him. But circumstances were such that only Donna could take the clear shot. She acted decisively and quickly and was accurate, or else he and Taylor would have been killed by Reed.

Weeks had passed since that traumatic night, and he finally realized that this was something he needed to do. He wanted to do it. Donna Gifford put herself in harm's way—even killed a man, though justly, to save his daughter and him. Even when you are on the right side of the law and end up killing the criminal, it has an effect on you forever. You never forget. He was so appreciative to Donna, and he needed to express that. How better than taking her to dinner?

Donna had been widowed for some time, and as she said, she hadn't been out for dinner socially with a member of the opposite sex for a long time. She had lived in Charlottesville, Virginia, and had just recently moved to the Akron area to live with her widowed mother and begin life anew. She had applied for a detective position at Conrad Confidential and was newly hired when she came to his assistance the night Reed had escaped. Barnabus Johnson, another newly hired detective, was present that evening as well, but it was Donna who took the shot and saved the day. And, yes, he was appreciative to Barnabus for being there for him when he didn't ask him to join them for the evening.

So was this a date as such? In Doug's mind, it was an appreciation dinner. That was his mind-set, but he still felt a little nervous. He certainly hadn't been on a date for over twenty-five years. Just going out with another woman other than Cynthia seemed awkward. He hadn't forgotten protocol or rules of etiquette, but it still seemed so *out of the box* for him.

He had washed his car by hand in the afternoon and cleaned the car on the inside as well. It was spotless. He had even loaded some soft, easy-listening CDs in the CD player. He didn't know what kind of music Donna liked, so he put in Cynthia's favorite ones—some Michael Bublé, Il Divo, Michael Bolton, Lionel Richie, and Whitney Houston.

He had Donna's address and used his GPS to find her house. He reviewed what he knew about her. Donna had been married to Pete for twenty years when he died of pancreatic cancer ten months after the diagnosis. Donna had worked for the Charlottesville Police Department and had been on their SWAT team. She had a black belt in judo, and as he recalled, she proved her proficiency in the interview. As he thought about that, he smiled. It took guts for her to flip him during a role-playing scenario he was merely setting up. She had a background in behavioral science and profiling. He also remembered how sensitive and tender she was with Wendy Graves on one of their more recent cases. Her fiancé, Andy Chandler, had committed suicide and Donna still went to Macy's department store to check up on her.

Donna's mother's name was Stella, and she was seventy-five years old. While Stella was still a healthy lady, Donna was still very attentive to her needs and desiring to help out in any way she could. She was very close to her mother. Both being widowed, they only had each other, so it seemed to be a good fit.

Doug arrived at the medium-sized ranch home. The yard was perfectly manicured. He was about five minutes early. He walked up to the front door and rang the doorbell. He straightened his tie and gave his pant legs and shoes one quick glance. He thought he heard a little commotion in the house—perhaps someone talking. Donna answered the door and invited him in. She was wearing a tailored black skirt that came to mid knee and a classy, form-fitting red-and-black jacket with a solid red shell under it. She stepped aside and introduced him to her mother, Stella, who was also a very attractive lady. Stella was quite petite and had snow-white hair. She had on a bright blue sweat suit and tennis shoes.

A rather large black and tan German shepherd weighing approximately sixty pounds and twenty-four inches tall walked into the room and immediately made its way to Doug.

"Don't worry, Doug. She's friendly. This is Blaze, my dog. He's six years old and was trained to work with me in Charlottesville. He sheds quite a bit, so be careful."

"What was he trained for?" Doug asked.

"He learned to follow scents, tracking criminals and cadaver searching. He learned to patrol troubled areas. He did narcotics and explosive detections and was trained for search and rescue. He was magnificent, but he's retired now. He went everywhere with me."

"Sounds like he's highly intelligent."

"He is. He has a very loyal nature. He can be a little overly protective at times, but he's very obedient. When on duty with me, he was fearless. It was an awesome experience working with Blaze," she remarked with great pride, as she patted Blaze on the head.

"I'm ready, Doug. I just need to go get my purse and a sweater." With that she exited the room.

"I made some cookies today, Mr. Conrad. I packaged a dozen or two for you. Let me go get them." Stella turned and made her way into what apparently was the kitchen.

"How nice, Mrs. LaMarre. Thank you."

Doug looked down on the floor and saw a large chewed-up rawhide bone. He picked it up to see if Blaze would take it, and then he heard the most massive deep sound, a baby gate fall over in another room, and coming at him at full speed was a 130-pound Dogue de Bordeaux, also known as a Bordeaux Mastiff. He was powerfully built, his large nostrils were puffing open, and his ears were straight up. It had the largest head of any canine Doug had ever seen. He had seen this breed only once before—in the movie *Turner and Hooch*. Before he could do or say anything, the dog had knocked him over, and he was lying on his back on the living room floor, straddled by this most intimidating dog. Doug let out a holler but still trying to appear manly.

"Uh . . . I need some help!"

Stella heard the commotion and, knowing immediately what had happened, rushed back into the living room, met by Donna. Donna was aghast at the sight.

The dog was drooling on Doug's face and shirt. Its face was only inches away from Doug's. Doug looked quite afraid. After all, he was used to having Snuggles, a twelve-pound shih tzu in his home, nothing like this big moose.

"Oh, Doug. I'm so sorry. I guess you've met Chunx," and with that, she firmly told Chunx to get off Doug. Thankfully, the dog obeyed her command.

"Mom, I thought he was confined to the kitchen," said Donna with a frustrated tone.

"Oh, Doug, I'm so sorry. Are you all right? I'll get a wet cloth and towel. Are you all right?" she kept asking with a sympathetic tone.

Doug got quickly to his feet. His heart was pounding, and slobber was everywhere on the front of his suit. He remained calm, but once again, he found himself alone in the room with this frightening canine.

"Chunx! Get over here!"

The dog obeyed and went to Stella promptly. As soon as he crossed into the kitchen, Stella put the baby gate up again.

"I'm so sorry, honey. I came to the kitchen to get the cookies I made for Mr. Conrad. I thought I had the baby gate secured. Chunx was just sitting there calmly, looking out into the living room. I don't know what made him knock the gate down and charge at him."

"Doug, maybe you better step into the guest bathroom and clean up a little. Here is the washcloth and towel for you."

"I never even saw Chunx until he was coming at me. I guess my back was turned from where he was. I had picked up the rawhide bone and was getting ready to entice Blaze to come to me when I heard a crashing sound and turned just in time to see Chunx charging at me. There was no time to—"

"That was Chunx's rawhide bone, and he won't let anyone mess with his bone—and definitely will he not share it with Blaze. He's more than a little territorial with his toys and snacks. I thought, however, that we had him secured in our kitchen so nothing like this would happen. I was going to introduce you to Chunx before we left—under the right circumstances, but . . . well . . . I hope you'll forgive him, Doug, and give Chunx another chance to be your friend. He really is a very sweet dog."

"Well, for sure I'd rather be his friend than his enemy," declared Doug as he wiped some of the massive doggie drool off his suit lapel with the damp cloth Donna had given him.

"Okay. I think I'm all cleaned up now. I'm ready whenever you are." As Doug stepped into the hall wide-eyed, he looked in both directions, no doubt checking for doggie appearances, specifically Chunx's.

Donna tried to stifle a smile.

"Have a good evening you two," said Stella with such sweet sincerity.

"Thanks! And thanks for the cookies. Sorry about the bone, Chunx. Promise not to touch it again!"

CHAPTER 11

Waneda Robinson had been widowed for nearly eighteen years. She had managed to keep up with the yard work since her husband of forty-eight years had died, but as time went on, it was becoming increasingly more difficult. Arthritis had set in, making it impossible to bend over and rake up the leaves from the two large maple trees she had in her back yard in the fall. Her grandson offered to do it occasionally, but he was busy with school sports and wasn't always available to help her out. Her house sat on three quarters of an acre of land and on the corner of a small road and a rather busy thoroughfare that took people from Barberton, Ohio, to Coventry Township. Over the years, as the area built up, it could be difficult pulling out onto the main road.

One day as she was out in her yard emptying a Japanese beetle bag and pinching some of her dried up geraniums, a young man pulled up in an old pickup truck alongside her house. He had light brown hair and was of medium stature. There was nothing that appeared sinister, so she stood there and waited for him to come to her.

"Hello, ma'am. I have passed this way for years going to work, but I lost my job due to the economy and downsizing and have noticed you doing some pretty heavy work all by yourself. I'm wondering if you could use some help. I'm willing to help you do outside or inside work for a fair price. I could sure use the work right now. I'm a pretty good mechanic and can fix most things."

"Where did you work?" asked Waneda.

"I worked at a lumber company."

"Carter Jones?" asked Waneda.

"Let's just say it was a competitor," answered Bobby.

Waneda wondered why he couldn't just give her the name of his company. Why did he have to *"let's just say . . ."*

"What is your name?" Waneda asked.

"Eugene Fielder, but my friends call me Gene." Of course Bobby wasn't about to reveal his real name.

"Well, why don't you give me your name and phone number and I'll give you a call if I need your help. I just completed most of the yard work that needs done right now, but I'm sure I could use you at a later time."

"Why don't I just stop by later and check up on you. Right now I don't have a phone where I can be reached. I've had to cut some corners in order to save money. I have a wife and a young baby to support. I've been looking quite a long time for a job, but companies just aren't hiring, as you probably already know."

"Well, I wish I could help you, but I wish you luck," said Waneda.

"Well, thanks anyway, ma'am. I'll stop by another time if I don't find a full-time job. Bobby got back in his truck and drove off. He saw the old lady watching him as he looked into his rearview mirror. He could see she wasn't buying into his story. He thought he was so credible, but the look on her face told him she was skeptical right from the get-go. He thought most ladies her age were supposed to be gullible. He just needed to be patient. He would keep trying different homes as he reviewed the obituaries and knew where the widows and widowers lived. Women were much easier to schnook-er than men. They were usually pretty easy targets. Today was not his lucky day, but without arousing too much suspicion, he might try this lady one more time a little later on.

As the young man drove away, Waneda had mixed feelings. She was on a fixed budget, but she also felt sorry for all these young people who were losing their jobs and had no income coming in at all, especially if they had families to support as this man said he had. But there was something about this guy—his body language or demeanor—that just didn't seem quite on the up-and-up. Her antennas went up about this guy. She wasn't quite sure why, but she knew she didn't have to hire him, so she respected her sixth sense, or woman's intuition, and figured that her husband would have been pleased with her foresight and prudence. Yes, she could certainly use some help, but this guy wasn't the one.

Waneda went inside her house and called her dear friend, Clare, to see if she was going to go to Bible study at their church on Thursday morning. Waneda was describing all the yard work she had been doing all day and had briefly mentioned this young man, Gene Fielder, who had stopped by looking for some work. Clare thought she had probably made the wrong decision as Waneda's back had been hurting her for months and she could certainly use some help. It was like God had dropped this guy on her doorstep as an answer to her problems, and she ignored it. Waneda had second thoughts then about her decision. If this young man stopped by again, she would probably take him up on his offer. There were certain jobs inside the house that needed attention, and the outside work seemed to be endless.

CHAPTER 12

Chris Lambert headed out to her mailbox after having seen their loyal mailman deliver the mail ten minutes before. Chris was the thirty-two-year-old daughter of a Summit County deputy sheriff who had always emphasized to her how important it was to be observant regarding her surroundings, so from a young age on, she truly had been an observant person, far exceeding the average person's norm.

She noticed her next-door neighbor, Mrs. Lawrence, talking to a rather young man in her driveway. She never got a glimpse of his face as he was facing away from her. A black truck was parked about ten feet from where they were standing. There was no insignia on the side of his truck to advertise his business, but he was dressed like a worker. It appeared the man was about to leave. She saw him shake hands with Mrs. Lawrence, and then he got in his truck and drove away. Chris watched with a bit of curiosity as Mrs. Lawrence waved good-bye to the man.

Chris was walking back to her house, flipping through her mail when she saw Mrs. Lawrence wave to her. Mrs. Lawrence was the sweetest eighty-year-old woman Chris had ever known. She was always happy, always upbeat and positive, and always enjoyed talking to people. She was the grandmotherly type, and Chris tried to keep a watchful eye out for Mrs. Lawrence.

As she walked close enough for hearing distance, Chris asked, "What's up, Mrs. L?"

"Oh, nothing much. I guess I may be getting a new roof soon."

"Oh, yeah. What's wrong with the one you've got?"

"Well, I didn't think anything, but this nice young man happened to be a roofer, and when he drove by, he saw that my roof was bowed in one spot."

"Really? Where?" asked Chris.

"He pointed to a spot, but I couldn't really see it. My eyes aren't too good these days, I'm afraid."

Chris looked at Mrs. L's roof—taking it all in and at different angles and couldn't see a problem whatsoever. Of course, she wasn't a roofer, nor did she have a roofer's eye. Everything looked fine to her.

"How old is your roof, Lois?" Chris rarely called Mrs. Lawrence by her first name.

"I think Harold replaced it shortly before he died thirteen years ago. I think he did, anyway. Oh, I can't remember. It seems so long ago."

"Well, usually roofs have a twenty-five—or thirty-year guarantee. Do you remember which company put your roof on? Perhaps they could come out and inspect it, and if there is a warranty, they would repair any damage for free."

"Well, I'm sure the roof does have a problem. He came in to the house to look at my ceiling where he saw the roof bowing, and he found a soft spot there. He said that usually means water leakage."

"Did this man have a business card, Mrs. L?"

"No, he said he'd call me back to follow up and see what I thought. He was such a nice young man. He and his brother have been doing roofs for the past ten years. In fact, he said they just did two houses right on our street, just around the bend. Those neighbors called him to replace their roofs after they had been damaged from a recent storm."

"What storm was that?" asked Chris as she was trying to recall a bad storm they just recently had.

"Well, I'm not sure I remember which one, but he said we had heavy rains, strong winds, and hail."

"Recently? Really?" Chris was pensive as she tried to recall this so-called recent storm.

"Well, yes. He isn't putting any pressure on me, and I know he's just trying to help me out. He's such a sweet young man who's just trying to eke out a living too, Chris."

"I get that, Mrs. L, but—what was this guy's name?

"Joe. He didn't say his last name that I recall, but he said he would supply references. He requires cash up front and would give me a significant senior citizens' discount if I paid him in cash. He said he would just charge me $15,000."

"That seems pretty cheap, Mrs. L, for the size of your house, but free would be even better if it was found to be under warranty. I think you should first get a second opinion before making a decision," advised Chris.

"That sounds reasonable, dear. Thanks for the advice."

"You bet! Don't forget to get your mail in, and have a good day, Mrs. Lawrence!" Chris said as she walked back to her house.

"You too, Chris. It's always a joy talking to you, dear."

Lois knew Chris was right, but she had already given Joe the job. When you shake hands with the company representative, you clenched the deal. Joe and his brother would start the job tomorrow afternoon. Once she gave Joe and his brother the cash in the morning, they would go buy the shingles and deliver all the supplies necessary. The following day, the work would begin, and by the beginning of the next week, the new roof would be completed. This would be the last roof she would need in her lifetime.

Harold would be so pleased with me for the way I've managed to keep up with the house since he's been gone, Lois thought. With that, Lois readied herself to go to the bank.

CHAPTER 13

The host led Donna and Doug to a private booth in the corner of the restaurant's main room. Donna had never dined at Hyde Park Grille before. It was quite impressive. Romantic instrumental music was playing, delicately folded napkins were on the table, and the host unfolded Donna's and placed it on her lap. Doug was already placing his napkin on his lap as they were handed menus and assured a waiter would be right over to take their beverage order.

Once their drink order was taken, Donna commented on what a wonderful selection the restaurant was.

"I must admit it's been one of my favorites over the years. The food surpasses the atmosphere even. I think you will enjoy your meal."

"Well, I'm sure I will, but the company will be very nice too. As I said before, I haven't been out to eat with anyone in a place like this since Peter died. I must admit it evokes an emotion and so many memories that I never expected. I don't want to get emotional on you."

"No problem. I think the same thing is happening to me as well, Donna. We are kind of in the same place in our lives regarding the loss of our spouse. Starting over after so many years of being in a happy marriage leaves me feeling pretty vulnerable and uncertain.

"Let me just say that my loss could have been greater had you not come to work for me and actually come to my home the night Reed showed up to kill me and Taylor. I view that as divine intervention, and I will be forever grateful to you for saving both our lives."

"Thanks, Doug. Being trained and on the SWAT team in Charlottesville for all those years just allowed me to do what I had done many times before. I can't even imagine going through what you had been through. Losing a spouse to illness is one thing, but to lose a loved one because of a criminal act would be much harder to get over. Then when your case gets national attention, as yours did, it creates more issues. It took away your privacy at a time when you needed it most, but the world wept with you and your family, Doug. You know that. You weren't alone. The entire country prayed for you, for Cynthia, your kids. The support was there, so it wasn't all bad. The cards, the flowers, the gifts . . . you had to feel the love."

"Yes, I did. But none of it brought Cynthia back to me."

"And it never will, Doug. Our spouses are gone, but they will live in our hearts forever. Now, I guess, we have no other choice but to move on, enjoy the memories, surround ourselves with the other important people in our lives, and let God lead us forward until we see His plan for us." Donna had such a sweet sincere look on her face, and yet he saw her eyes were tearing. He understood what she was saying and couldn't have agreed more. She was such a nice, refreshing person, and in many ways, they had quite a bit in common with each other.

Both enjoyed their meals, followed by a decadent dessert. When the waiter described it as having chunks of chocolate surrounding it, both Doug and Donna smiled. Chunks. Chunx.

"You know, I was hoping your introduction to our sweet Chunx would have started off a little better. He really is a very sweet dog, but I must admit, you were so poised lying there on the floor with Chunx slobbering all over you."

"Well, let's face it. I didn't have much of a choice. To tell you the truth, I was scared to death. He is a muscular dog with impressive hanging jowls and nasty breath."

"I'm sure he was too close for comfort today. I'll work on his breath if you'll come back next week and join my mother and me for a homemade dinner. Maybe you and Chunx can have a second chance at becoming friends. What do you say?" Donna was smiling so sweetly, it would have been hard to resist her.

"All right. I'll be sure to bring him a rawhide bone and a squeaky he-man toy. Yeah?"

"That would be great!"

CHAPTER 14

It was ten o'clock in the morning when Joe called Lois Lawrence.

"Mrs. Lawrence, I was wondering if my brother, Dex, could stop by and pick up the money? I am heading out to Millersburg to pick up some of the roof supplies for you and another one of our customers and load it on the truck. It will save us considerable time and we can get started maybe even today on your roof."

"Yes, that would be fine, Joe. I have the money already here. What does your brother look like?"

"He's really ugly, Mrs. Lawrence. I'm the good-looking one. He's ugly, but he's the smart one, and he handles the financial end of the business. He should be there in about fifteen minutes or so."

"Okay. I'll see him when he gets here," she laughed. *Maybe I'll make some cookies for them today,* she thought. If Joe's brother is anything like him, it will be fun to have a few young men around the house. Her son had died at childbirth, but had he lived, he would probably have been about the age of Joe. She was looking forward to helping these young guys out and getting her roof done as well.

She heard a car door slamming and looked out the window to see a young man walking up to her side door. It must be Dex. Without any hesitation, she opened the door to let him in.

CHAPTER 15

Chris Lambert was returning home from a Saturday morning of grocery shopping and errand running. She had been to Target, Sally's Beauty Supply, Shaffer's Market, and ended her agenda at Giant Eagle. As she turned on her street, she saw police cars blocking the road, a medical examiner's van, and a crowd of neighbors huddled together on both sides of the road, talking. A few were even crying and hugging each other.

Chris slowed her Chrysler Town and Country van and realized the activity was at Mrs. L's house. A yellow crime tape had been placed around Mrs. Lawrence's property. She was able to pull in her driveway but wouldn't have been permitted to go further down the street as a police car was blocking the road. She quickly went inside her house, unloaded the groceries that contained the milk and ice cream, and quickly called out to her husband, Jerry. She got no reply.

She rushed out to the street to see what was happening. Jerry was coming toward her.

"Oh, my God, Jerry, what has happened? Is Mrs. Lawrence okay?"

"Chris, something awful has happened!"

"Is she dead?" asked Chris reticently.

"Yes, she is, honey."

"Heart attack? What? But why would there be crime—"

"She was shot to death," explained Jerry speedily but as tenderly as he could. He wanted to allay her questions and confusion and bring her up to speed with the rest of the neighborhood.

"Shot to death? Oh, Jerry, no. She couldn't have been. Lois Lawrence shot to death?"

"It's true, honey."

"When? Who would do this?" she asked as more questions were rushing to her head.

"They don't have a suspect yet, but apparently, word has it she's been dead for several days. Nobody knew."

"Who found her?"

"I heard Lana Cromley found her. Apparently she went over to give Mrs. Lawrence some of her mail that had been delivered to her mailbox by mistake, and when she rang the doorbell and Mrs. L never came to the door, Lana happened to peak through the window and saw her legs on the floor. It looked like she had fallen while in another room, near the doorway, and either couldn't get up or had collapsed. Lana called the police and paramedics immediately. They broke in and found her dead."

"So the doors were locked? So who shot her? Surely she didn't commit suicide?" asked Chris inquisitively and in total disbelief of that theory.

"No, they know it was murder. The police are tight-lipped, but they want to question the neighbors to see when she was last seen and help with a time frame, I guess. I'm sure they'll want to talk to you, Chris. You were probably closer to Mrs. L than anyone in the neighborhood."

"Yes, I probably am . . . was."

As Chris had time to process what happened, she began to cry.

"Why would anyone want to kill that poor lady? She never hurt anyone. How could anyone hurt such a sweet lady?" she moaned.

Jerry put his arms around Chris and just let her sob on his shoulders. Lois Lawrence was like a second mom to Chris for sure. This would leave an everlasting hole in Chris's heart. Until the neighbors learned more, fear and apprehension would build. Could this happen again in their peaceful neighborhood? Once the motive was known, it might put the neighbors at ease. Of course, that would mean that an arrest had been made as well, most likely.

As the neighbors conjectured, the economy and job losses were becoming so prevalent in the area, people were resorting to home burglaries. But why choose little old ladies on fixed incomes? Could they have possibly gotten that much from her? Had her house been ransacked?

Lana Cromley had not seen any disarray when she peaked through the window, but she only had a view of Mrs. L's foyer and a small part of her living room. Lana believed Mrs. L was lying face down based on the position of her legs and feet. If, indeed, that was true, Mrs. L had been shot in the back.

The entire neighborhood was trying to speculate on the case. What could Mrs. L have had that was so valuable that someone would kill her for? They wouldn't have needed to kill her for it. She would have likely surrendered it to them without a fight. Since there was no visible break-in, did she know the person or persons who did this? She seldom had company. She had outlived most of her family and friends. The neighbors had pretty much adopted her into their families. In fact, their kids called her grandma. She loved them, and they loved her. This would be poignant for the little ones especially. It was unimaginable to think that the kind of person Mrs. L was should die by way of violence. It was incongruous and unfair.

Surely the police will solve this quickly. It's for sure no one on Hyfield Street will sleep well until an arrest is made. Something just didn't feel right to Chris. She couldn't get her mind wrapped around what was bothering her, but maybe in time, it would come to her.

CHAPTER 16

The police had gone door to door and talked to each neighbor individually. They wanted to know when and where they had last seen Mrs. Lawrence. They asked them to tell what they knew about the lady, if they had seen anything unusual or suspicious in the last week or so. Had Mrs. Lawrence mentioned she was frightened or concerned about anything? Who were her friends and family members that she spent time with? Who were her visitors? Were there any neighbors Mrs. Lawrence didn't get along with? Are there any neighbors who are known to be belligerent, contrary, troublemakers, or unemployed and in need? Were there any known felons living in the neighborhood?

No one had seen or heard anything suspicious. The neighborhood was a close-knit group of people who did try to watch out for one another, even though they were all busy and active in their lives. Mrs. Lawrence was one of the most beloved neighbors. She was so kind and loving to the children and often sent cookies or cakes over to the neighbors. Everyone loved her. No one could even take a wild guess as to who might have killed her. Murders didn't happen in *their* neighborhood, and they really didn't as proven by the records.

When they got to the Lambert home, Chris met the police at the door and invited them in. It was obvious from her demeanor that she had been very close to Mrs. Lawrence. The Lambert home was right next door to Mrs. L's house. If anyone could see the comings and goings at Mrs. Lawrence's house, it would be the Lamberts. Chris was a stay-at-home Mom, so she would have been home at all hours of the day. Chris admitted that she was pretty attentive to Mrs. Lawrence because of her age. Chris described Mrs. Lawrence as a kind, caring lady who had the admiration and respect of the entire neighborhood. Any one of them would have stepped forward to protect Mrs. L if necessary.

When asked about Mrs. L's health, Chris replied that Mrs. L did pretty well for herself. She was able to fend for herself. She still drove and ran her own errands and still took pride in her house and yard. She hired a landscaping company to keep the trees pruned and to do the spring clean up, mow the lawn weekly, and gather up the fall leaves. Actually, Mrs. L did a better job than some of the young neighbors did. Chris actually bragged on Mrs. L's success like a proud daughter edifying her mother. When asked about any unemployed neighbors who might be in need of money, Chris asked the deputy if Mrs. Lawrence had been robbed?

"I'm sorry. We're not at liberty to say."

"Just askin', you understand." Chris put two and two together and surmised that Mrs. L had been robbed and that robbery may have been the motive.

"No, everyone around here is employed and doing pretty well, the best that I can tell."

The deputy thanked Chris for her time and told her if she could think of anything that might be useful to their investigation, she should call the Summit County Sheriff's office and ask for him. With that, he gave her his business card.

"I hope you catch the person or persons who did this, officer. She didn't deserve to die this way. We all want to see justice served here, plus it has made us all feel very uneasy about our own safety."

"We're doing our best, ma'am."

CHAPTER 17

Ruby Johnson, Barnabus Johnson's grandmother, had been gravely ill for several months and had just recently entered ICU at Akron General Medical Center.

Doug Conrad had learned Ruby had pretty much reared Barnabus. Why Barnabus's parents weren't in the picture was unknown, but clearly Ruby was his surrogate mother. Barnabus had spoken highly of her in conversations with him, and it was clear she was important to him. Ruby was seventy-eight years old, and he had constantly doted upon her. Of course, she had always done the same for him.

Doug told Barnabus to take as much time off as he felt he needed in order to care for his grandmother. He and Mitch would take over two of the cases he was working on by himself until Barnabus could return.

Barnabus had been hired by a man named Dan Bender. Apparently Mr. Bender's mother had been murdered months ago. The Summit County Sheriff's Department was working the case, but things were getting cold. Alexander Drew and his deputies had been so compassionate to Dan. He never questioned their efforts or sincerity, but things weren't moving quickly enough for him. Dan had found the name of Dexter Rabone scribbled on a Post-It in his mother's handwriting on the kitchen counter. He had never heard his mom mention anyone by that name, nor did he think she knew this person. Dan had told the police about the name, but they seemed disinterested and didn't think it would lead to anywhere but a dead end. Given the fact that prior to her death Mrs. Bender had withdrawn $50,000 from her savings account, Barnabus had checked first with her bank, Eastern Capitol, to see if anyone by that name worked there. No current or past employee with that name was listed. Barnabus, however, was continuing to track down that name.

The other case involved a teen whose parents suspected he was using and selling drugs. He had been drug tested at their family physician's office, but the tests came back negative. While they were pleased about that, they had found him with large sums of money that he couldn't explain where it came from. He didn't have an after-school job. Barnabus began to follow the kid after school and record his stops and who he was seeing before he returned home. Barnabus had concluded in his notes that something was looking suspicious, but he had no foolproof evidence as of yet. He was continuing the surveillance of the kid whose name was Ryan.

"We're doing our best, ma'am."

CHAPTER 18

W aneda Robinson had lived in Coventry Township for nearly fifty-eight years. She and her husband, who was now deceased for nearly eighteen years, put three children through the Coventry school district and then on to universities of their choice. Her oldest daughter graduated from Kent State University while the second daughter graduated from Bob Jones University in Greenville, South Carolina. Ten years later, her son, Terry, received his degree in engineering from the University of Akron. Like most families back then, the wives were stay-at-home moms and most dads worked in the rubber factories. The factory work was hard and tiring, but families worked together, made sacrifices, so that they could give their children opportunities they didn't have while growing up in the Depression years. They usually had backyard gardens and took pride in their middle class homes.

Terry had married a lovely young woman named Kathleen who had grown up in their church. Kathleen's mother, Clare Rouse, was a dear friend to Waneda for many years, long before their two children started dating. Both Waneda and Clare had lost their husbands in the same year and had become even closer friends. They met for lunch often, shared many family gatherings, and especially enjoyed meeting at Gospel Bible Church every Tuesday morning for women's Bible study.

From September to May, the women attending the study would have a luncheon at the church following the Bible study, but from June to August, many of the ladies would meet for lunch in some of the local restaurants. The summer meetings had fewer women than September to May's attendance because of family vacations or the women entertained out-of-town guests or just because they needed more time to get yard work done. Whatever the reasons and despite their busyness, there were still forty to fifty women who showed up for Tuesday's Bible study.

Gospel Bible was a very warm and inviting church made up of caring people. The pastor, Pastor Greg Myer, was truly loved by the congregation, and his wife, Sue, led the Bible study every week. She was an eloquent, articulate speaker and such a great teacher. What was even more admirable was her servant's heart to help others in need.

Clare Rouse's two grandchildren, Kaitlyn and Amanda, from her son, Jim, were also active in the church and were participants in the women's Bible study. Kaitlyn, the older granddaughter, was thirty-eight years old. She had two children in the fifth and sixth grades and was a stay-at-home mom. She had married well and was grateful a second job wasn't necessary to make ends meet. Amanda was twenty-six years old and had one child in first grade. She had married a highly successful architect, and it was decided she should remain a homemaker as well. Both girls had earned bachelor degrees in music, so it worked out beautifully that Kaitlyn would lead the ladies in some hymns and would arrange special music each week before Sue stepped up to the podium and presented her lesson. She always tried to tie the words of the songs to the theme of Sue's lesson for that week.

Amanda played the piano and organ and oftentimes favored the ladies with a flute solo while Kaitlyn would back her up on piano. Clare could not have been prouder of her grandchildren.

So while Gospel was a rather small, intimate church, it was a *doing* church, filled with talented people. It had also been growing in attendance. So much so that plans for expanding the building had begun. Amanda's husband who owned his own architectural firm had been hired for the job.

Stella LaMarre, Donna Gifford's mother, was also good friends with Waneda Robinson and Clare Rouse. Most of the time Waneda would drive to Stella's house as it was on the way to Gospel, and they would take turns driving to the Bible study together.

Clare, on the other hand, would stop at Ridgewood Place, a nursing home, and pick up Gracie Holstrom. Gracie was ninety-five years old. She had attended Gospel for many, many years. In fact, she had attended long before Pastor Greg and Sue had come to the church.

Gracie was probably no taller than four feet eleven and couldn't weigh more than ninety pounds wringing wet. Her mind was still sharp as was her hearing. Her eyesight, however, was poor, and she needed assistance walking. She had two bottom teeth in the front of her mouth and never seemed to be wearing her false teeth. At one time, she had owned some. When Clare inquired about them to Ridgewood Place, it was clear the teeth had disappeared with no explanation. Stolen? Accidentally picked up with old papers on her side table and thrown away? No one knew. Gracie had outlived her husband and two sons, so the church people took responsibility for watching over her.

Gracie was a stalwart of the church and was endeared by everyone there. Everyone was protective of this dear, sweet, spiritual lady. Despite her age and having been put in a nursing home by distant relatives, Gracie was one of the happiest ladies Clare had ever known. She had wisdom and deep discernment, and everyone dreaded the day when there would no longer be Gracie Holstrom in their lives. She had touched their lives like no other human being. Even the young children of the church gravitated to her. Gracie always had a hug and kiss for the children. She was everybody's grandma.

CHAPTER 19

B obby and Eddie knew that in all of their schemes, patience and follow-through were important. That's what accounted for their successful scams. They tried never to appear pushy or too aggressive with their victims. They tried never to arouse suspicion or skepticism either. If one of their targets got too inquisitive, it could spell *big* trouble. They had always made a point of doing two or three scams and then leaving the area, sometimes even the state. They would lie low for a while, pull a few more here and there, and, again move on. The trail was always cold. They both had several fake IDs they used when staying at cheap motels to add confusion to anyone who might wish to pursue them.

Because Eddie and Bobby traded off following their victims, the target never seemed to catch on. Of course, they targeted the older people who were forgetful and typically oblivious to their surroundings. If by chance they found the elderly person to be sharper than they had previously thought, they walked away from that potential victim. There was too much at stake to get caught, and so many other victims were out there who were perfect preys. So patience was vital as they scrutinized each person regardless whether they were male or female.

Bobby, however, couldn't put Waneda Robinson out of his mind. She seemed to really need help with her yard, but when he approached her, she had surprised him by interviewing him. She asked a lot of questions that forced him to lie. He had a lot of different lies he told to each of his victims, so he had to keep his stories straight and not provide them with anything they could look into. Most of the time, it worked like a charm. He sensed Waneda Robinson was suspicious of him, so common sense told him to leave her alone and simply walk away. Neither he nor Eddie liked being outsmarted by the elderly. Eventually, those people will leave their guard down at some point, and they can take advantage of them.

Waneda looked to be in her eighties, but she was spry. They knew she had children that dropped in to see her throughout the week, and they certainly didn't want to be at the house when they were there. They figured if they followed Mrs. Robinson for a while, she might lead them to some of her elderly friends who could be *good victims*.

They learned after following her for several weeks that she seldom left her house. She went to the grocery store and the hair salon mostly. But they did learn she went to church on Tuesday mornings, and lots of old ladies were going into the building too. No men. That got their attention.

Eddie was the *brainchild* and decided to inquire about what was going on inside the church. It looked like it might be an opportunity beyond their wildest imagination.

Eddie went to a pay phone and looked up the church's phone number and then dialed.

"Gospel Bible Church. How may I direct your call?" said a young, friendly female voice.

"I have an elderly mother who has come to stay with me for a while, and I think she's getting bored staying at my house while I'm at work. I'm not a church attendee, but she is. Do you have any activity through the week that might fit the bill for her?"

"Well, on Tuesday mornings we have the Women's Bible Study at 10:00 a.m. We have about fifty ladies who attend. It lasts for one hour, usually, and then they dismiss. Some of the ladies go home, but many of the ladies go out to lunch together and have a really good time."

"What is the age range of the ladies because my mom is in her eighties?" Eddie asked sincerely.

"Oh, she'll fit in just fine. Most of the ladies are in their seventies and eighties. We even have one who is ninety-five years old. Mrs. Myer, the Bible study teacher who is also our pastor's wife, is in her late forties, and our song director and our pianist are in their twenties, so there are a few younger ones."

"My mom doesn't like crowds—she avoids them every chance she gets. Are there other people or groups at the church at that time?" Eddie asked.

"No. The men's groups meet on Saturday mornings. Of course, our pastor is in and out of the building throughout the day, and then I'm on the switchboard every day, so that's about it. She should do well here. All the ladies are so sweet, and I'm sure they'd befriend your mom immediately and make her feel comfortable. If you want me to, I can meet her at the door and escort her into the sanctuary and introduce her to some of the ladies. What is her name?"

"How about I talk to her about this first, and if she's willing to come, I'll call you again and give you her name so you can meet her at the door?" Eddie said in his most cooperative tone.

"Sure. We'd love to have her. You make sure she knows that."

"Will do. Thanks for the information. I'll pass it along to Mom."

As soon as Eddie hung the phone up, he knew what their final scam in Akron would be. It would be their biggest one yet perhaps. It might then be time to cross the border for a while.

CHAPTER 20

Eddie Flatt never in his entire life displayed initiative. He never wanted a job or a career, but he did want a paycheck, so he would listen to shysters in bars and learned how to screw over innocent victims. It didn't take long to learn that the best targets were old, unhealthy people. They are so trusting and naïve. Eddie had played around with drug dealing for a while, but he learned quickly that you eventually get caught and end up in prison. Once the police know you and you have a record, there is always a paper trail. A successful scam artist leaves no paper trail or evidence.

Bobby never used drugs, even when Eddie tried to entice his friend to smoke a joint with him on occasion. Eddie never got into drugs in a big way either. His vice was buying *guy toys*—sports and hunting equipment, animal traps. He wanted *things*. Neither he nor Bobby grew up having anything, but some day, they both agreed they would get rich and own a mansion, nice cars, and have things that would earn people's respect and, of course, attract the chicks. They would show all the college-educated, hardworking pigs that they could obtain wealth faster and easier without breaking a sweat. This month they had earned a bonanza through their ruses. One more was left in their pocket of tricks, and then they would quickly leave town and probably never return. While this was their hometown, they had no family or friends to speak of, so it wouldn't be that great of a loss for them.

Eddie was the ringleader of the two. He and Bobby had driven to Gospel Bible Church at least four times late at night to scope the layout of the church. They knew there were five different doors that led inside the building. Two were glass doors that they could see in and get a good idea as to where they might lead to. Two clearly led into the main sanctuary. One was a hallway with doors on both sides. Bobby figured they led to Sunday school classes and perhaps a nursery. One seemed to lead to private offices. Venetian blinds on some of the windows were closed so that they couldn't be sure.

They spent several hours mapping out their strategy until they had devised a unique plan that could net them a considerable amount of money. It was a bold plan, but they were counting on the element of surprise, the ladies' gripping fear that they would instill in them immediately to gain their cooperation, and finally their lack of technology and slow reactions to make their ruse work. Eddie and Bobby reviewed their roles over and over. They worked through different scenarios should something go wrong or contrary to plan. They felt confident they had covered all of the bases.

One dramatic phone call needed to be made before they would move into action. They had been parked across the street observing the church's parking lot for over forty minutes, seeing who was coming and going. They counted the number of women entering the building and couldn't help but notice how many walked with canes or walkers or were assisted by other women. All, however, were carrying purses. The walls of Jericho were about to come down.

CHAPTER 21

As Meg was finishing typing Reverend Myer's notes for Sunday's sermon, the phone rang. She answered before the second ring.

"Gospel Bible Church. This is Meg Foster. How may I help you?"

Bobby replied, "I'm having some serious problems in my life right now, and I wondered if I could speak to the pastor?"

"I'm sorry. Pastor Myer is conducting a funeral right now and I don't expect him back before 3:00 p.m. Could I—"

"Well, is there any other male there in your church who might be able to give me some advice right now?" Bobby asked in a sincere voice.

"I'm sorry, there isn't. Our pastor's wife is leading the ladies' Bible study in the sanctuary. She'll be finished in about an hour. Would you be willing to speak to her?"

"No. I really need to get some advice from a man. I may call back later."

"Well, would you like to leave your name and phone number, and I could have Pastor Myer call you?"

"No. No, thank you."

Bobby immediately disconnected and informed Eddie that there were no men in the building nor would there be until three o'clock.

It was the last piece of information they needed before initiating their plan. They both looked at each other and smiled.

"Well, then, let's roll, good buddy!" said Eddie.

With their pickup truck, they drove over and parked on the side of the church that could not be seen by travelers passing the front of the building. They grabbed their large, oversized gym bags filled with five

Kryptonite Evolution Mini U-locks to secure the church doors. No one could get in or out with those locked on the doors. The security rating was 9 out of 12; they had 13 millimeter max-performance steel shackles that resist bolt cutters and leverage attacks and had reinforced cuffs over a crossbar and cylinder for added security. And they had a box of Iron Hold heavy-duty 55 gallon contractor bags to carry their plunder away.

They were ready to get down to business.

CHAPTER 22

All the ladies had made their way into the sanctuary and found their usual seats. Sue Myer, sitting on the platform, looked out at her audience and knew where to look to find each one of her loyal ladies. They were certainly creatures of habit. Some sat with their mom, sister, cousins, or neighbors each week. Some sat with a special friend, but always they sat in the same pew. Most of these ladies attended Gospel Bible, and the other fourth had been invited here long ago by one of the members, enjoyed the Bible study, and loved the sweet fellowship. Sue had come to know them very well since they had become regular attendees.

Sue knew that Edith Mayer wouldn't be there. She had flown to Chicago to be with her daughter who was expecting twins any day, but it looked like everyone else was in attendance. There didn't seem to be any new faces present.

Yes, Sue knew all of these ladies. Each one had a story, a history, and had at one time or another given her personal testimony to this group of women. As she looked out at the sea of faces, she looked quickly to make sure Gracie Holstrom was in the room. After all, Gracie was ninety-five years old and getting more fragile with every passing year. Gracie had outlived her husband and both of her sons. Gracie's youngest son had been a policeman and had been hit by a drunk driver while directing traffic on Route 8 after a three-vehicle crash. Her oldest son had been killed in the Vietnam War at age 21. Both losses were hard on her and Herb, but Gracie redirected her affections on other children. She and Herb did volunteer work at Akron Children's Hospital. They were involved in many fund-raisers to help the families of veterans and fallen police officers. Gracie taught Sunday school and vacation Bible school for over thirty years in the church. She had been married to Herb for sixty-two years, but after Herb died, Sue saw the vitality leave Gracie. Her health began to decline, but she always seemed jovial and never complained about her health or her losses or her loneliness. She wore a smile on her face, but the twinkle in her eye was missing when children weren't around her. She knew Gracie walked a close walk with God every day. You couldn't help but love Gracie. She was truly special to anyone who knew her, and especially to these ladies.

Sue's eyes landed on Olga Banks who was struggling with breast cancer and then on Fannie Furman who had cared for her Down's syndrome daughter for over forty years. It was becoming more difficult to keep up with the care needed as Fannie was in her late seventies. Then there was Olivia Rainey who had struggled with drug addiction. She had taken painkillers after having back surgery and somehow lost control. She had been in rehab too many times to count. Greg had visited her many times in the drug unit and had prayer with her. Her recovery has been a slow process, but Sue was sure she would come out victoriously.

Addie Bartow had been married almost thirty-five years to an abusive husband. She didn't believe in divorce, but her last beating almost cost her her life. Ben ended up in prison, and she finally sought a divorce. She still struggled with guilt, unworthiness, and constant pain from the many fractures she endured from the beatings.

Yes, Sue could go on and on about each one, but the bottom line was that everyone in the room needed the Lord. Sue was so committed to teaching these wonderful ladies and took her responsibility very seriously. They've all come together in one place to praise and thank the Lord for His love and protection and to edify one another. This morning she had a great lesson in God's Word that should uplift and bring confidence to each heart.

Kaitlyn Kidwell, Clare Rouse's granddaughter, walked to the podium and spoke into the microphone.

"Well, good morning, ladies! Why don't we all stand while Amanda starts us on our first song of the day."

Amanda, Kaitlyn's younger sister, played the chorus on the organ all the way through and then played the introduction.

"All right, ladies, let's lift up our voices!"

Nothing is impossible when you put your trust in God;
Nothing is impossible when you're trusting in His word.
Hearken to the voice of God to thee;
Is there anything too hard for me?
Then put your trust in God alone and rest upon His word,
For everything, O everything, yes everything is possible with
God!

As soon as the chorus was completed, Kaitlyn told the ladies they could sit down but that she still wanted them to sing out as they turned in their hymnals in front of them to page 70.

Amanda began playing the introduction when her sister gave her the nod.

"We will sing the first three verses of this song. Kaitlyn lifted her hands and brought them back down indicating for the song to begin:

Rescue the perishing, Care for the dying,
Snatch them in pity from sin and the grave,
Weep o'er the erring one, Lift up the fallen,
Tell them of Jesus the mighty to save.

Tho' they are slighting Him, Still He is waiting,
Waiting the penitent child to receive.
Plead with them earnestly, Plead with them gently,
He will forgive, if they only believe.

Down in the human heart, Crushed by the tempter,
Feelings lie buried that grace can restore,
Touched by a loving heart, Weakened by kindness,
Chords that are broken will vibrate once more.

Rescue the perishing, Care for the dying; Jesus is
Merciful, Jesus will save.

As soon as the song ended, Sue traded places with Kaitlyn and read several verses in the Bible, which would be their text for today. They would focus on those scriptures in about ten minutes, right after a few announcements, prayer, and a testimony.

"I'm reading from John 15:5

I am the vine, ye are the branches. He that abideth in me and I in him, the same bringeth forth much fruit; for without me, ye can do nothing.

"Now verse 9:

As the Father hath loved me, so have I loved you; continue in my love.

"And finally verse 13:

Greater love hath no man than this, that a man lay down his life for his friends.

Sue asked the ladies to bow their heads for a word of prayer. Every head was bowed and every eye closed as Sue prayed for Edith Mayer's daughter as she was about to deliver twins. She prayed for the Murdoch family who had lost their mother, leaving three teenage sons behind. Greg would be conducting her funeral in about thirty minutes. Sue thanked God for His Word—a book of truth that has the power to comfort every heavy heart in the room and was the holy, authoritative standard for our lives. It is the benchmark for evaluating everything, she declared. As soon as she said Amen, she lifted her head as did all of the other ladies, and much to their surprise, two men were in their midst with some serious-looking guns pointing directly at them.

CHAPTER 23

As soon as Eddie and Bobby had the attention of every lady in the room, Eddie spoke out.

"All right. Listen up, ladies, and listen well and nobody gets hurt."

He turned to Sue who stood frozen at the pulpit and the two younger ladies sitting on the chairs on the stage.

"All three of you, go sit on the front row with the other ladies."

Amanda and Kaitlyn reached beside their chairs to take their purses with them.

"Leave them where they are girls. That is what our brief little meeting is all about. Now get to the front row."

Sue turned to wait for the girls so she would be behind the girls, but Eddie pushed her toward the steps. Sue lost her balance and fell. The women in the congregation gasped loudly for fear Sue was hurt. She quickly got up, followed by Amanda and Kaitlyn who looked terrified. The three ladies sat close together on the first row in the center pew.

Eddie nodded at Bobby who then took off down a side hall locking the side doors from the inside with their special locks. He was then in pursuit to bring the receptionist, Meg Foster, whom they believed was the only person in the building to the sanctuary to join the other ladies.

Once Bobby had secured all of the doors, he found the office and saw Meg Foster sitting at her computer, focusing on her monitor. She didn't see or hear him step into the office until he was upon her. He aimed the gun directly at her, and she froze with utter fear.

"I want all of the money you have stored here in the church—NOW!" he screamed with a demanding tone.

"We don't have any. It was deposited in the bank Sunday after the service was over. We don't keep any money here through the week."

"If you're lying to me, lady, you're dead!"

"No, I'm telling the truth. Please, please don't hurt me. I swear I'm telling the truth."

"Give me your purse," Bobby ordered.

She opened her desk drawer and handed him her purse.

"Now move. We're going to the sanctuary to join the other women."

Meg noticed as they passed one of the side doors that he had some kind of heavy-duty lock on the doors so that no one could get out. It would also mean that no one could enter either.

Whoever this guy was, she thought, he's not taking a chance for an escape—or rescue. Her mind quickly went to the day she had accepted the job at Gospel. One of the pluses for the job was that it would be a safe working environment. She never dreamed she would find herself in this predicament. These kinds of things happen to other people, but not to her.

When she stepped into the sanctuary, they had entered through the front of the room. All of the women were seated with shocked looks on their faces. Another man with a gun was standing in front and giving the ladies a directive. How many bad guys were there, she wondered.

"Now, ladies, I want you all to pass your purses to your right—to the end of every row—and we'll be taking them with us. If anyone even attempts to grab a cell phone or call for help or remove one thing from your purse, you will get a bullet through your head. This ordeal will be over swiftly and be uneventful if you follow our directions and cooperate."

Waneda who was sitting next to Stella whispered quietly, "Oh, my god. I think I recognize the one guy. His name is Eugene Fielder. He came to my home looking for work."

Before the man had spoken those words, Stella had already taken her cell phone out of her pocket and was quickly texting her daughter, Donna, for help. Stella didn't even own a cell phone until Donna came to live with her and insisted she carry one on her at all times, just in case of an emergency. Donna even insisted she learn to text. It was painful and laborious, but Donna finally taught her to text. Never once did she ever dream she would have to text in an attempt to save her life.

Stella had no idea when Donna would check her text messages, but Donna had asked her mom to text her when Bible study was almost over and she would meet her, Waneda, Clare, and Gracie for a quick lunch at Ruby Tuesday's, so Donna would be checking sometime soon. She just didn't know if she would see the text in time to call for help.

Donna had even insisted that she learn to text quickly. Stella never got too good at speed, but she learned the shortcuts. Hopefully, she wouldn't get caught with her cell phone on her. She had quickly sent her message:

2 mn w/ guns @ church, stlg purs, recog 1 ugene feelder call 911

Stella then slipped her cell phone down her blouse into her bra as inconspicuously as she could. It was on vibration but not on sound. Hopefully, Donna would trust her mom and not try to call her back. If she got caught with the cell phone, she feared this guy would do what he said he would do.

As Stella was passing her purse over to Clare and watched it continuing down the line of women, she whispered to Clare, "Waneda recognizes the one man. She's pretty sure he's the one who recently stopped at her house wanting to help with the yard work. He said his name was Eugene Fielder."

Clare looked straight ahead while Stella was talking to her, not wanting to arouse attention. If Waneda was correct in the man's identification and if this was a simple robbery with a good outcome, these men would get caught. If somehow things went awry, Clare worried not so much for herself but for her two beautiful granddaughters sitting in the front row. She also worried about all of her friends, and of course, she felt a huge responsibility for Gracie.

If Stella was able to get a quick message to Donna and Donna was able to receive it quickly and call the police, it was possible help would be here in minutes. No matter how this played out, it was going to be a very interesting day for about fifty ladies.

CHAPTER 24

Donna Gifford was on hold with a client when her iPhone buzzed. She looked down and saw a message from her mother. It was a little earlier than she had anticipated. She couldn't believe what she read. She read it one more time.

The women at the church were getting robbed of their purses at gunpoint? And her mom knew one of the gunmen? Eugene Fielder? Who was he? She didn't recognize the name and had never heard her mother mention anyone by that name.

One thing Donna knew was that her mother would never lie about something like this. She quickly called the sheriff's office and reported her mom's text message. She was told they would send two cars out immediately. They were aware weapons might be involved so they would be alert and progress accordingly. They would be ready to ask for back up if necessary as well.

Donna feared if she texted her mom, the gunmen might hear the vibration, but she texted anyway. Donna grabbed her gun and purse and stopped by Mitch Neubauer's office. Barnabus had been out of the office for two days as his grandmother was gravely ill and probably dying, and Doug Conrad was out working a case. She let Mitch know what was happening.

"I'm heading for the church right now, Mitch," she said with urgency. The police are on their way too. Let Doug know where I am. I'm not sure just how serious this is, but I don't like the sound of it. My mom is in that church. I lost Pete too early, and I don't intend to lose my mother too."

"I'll call Doug and let him know. Keep in touch with us, Donna. If there's anything we can do, we'll be there."

Mitch had wished he could help in a more physical way, but since Quinton Reed's attack on him, he had not yet recovered from his physical injuries. In fact, he may never fully recover. He had physical limitations, but it hadn't prevented him from the investigative work required on the job.

Doug was at Dan Bender's home receiving some of the facts regarding Dan's mother's murder when he got Mitch's call. He stepped out of the client's home to speak privately with Mitch.

"It seems Donna's mother is at Gospel Bible Church for a ladies' Bible study when two men walked in and at gunpoint are attempting to steal their purses. It seems Stella recognizes one of the guys and was able to identify him as Eugene Fielder.

"How would she know this guy?" asked Doug.

"We don't know that yet. Donna doesn't recognize the name or recall her mother ever mentioning that name."

"Has Donna received any more texts from Stella?"

"No. She was probably just lucky to get that one off without getting caught, but she clearly believes the women are in danger. Donna quickly texted her mom back, but she doesn't know if she was able to read it."

"What did Donna write?"

"Just told her to keep her phone in hiding and cooperate with the gunmen."

"I'm on my way to the church now, Mitch. See what you can find out about that Eugene Fielder. By the way, call Barnabus and just let him know what's going on with Donna's mother. We don't expect him to leave his grandmother, but we don't want him feeling left out when it comes to things that affect our team."

"You got it, Doug. Hopefully, this will turn out to be nothing. I'll check out Fielder and get back with you."

Doug suddenly had a flashback; he pictured Cynthia running into the woods—running for her life and then getting shot in the back just before help arrived. This time it was a member of Donna's family who was in harm's way. Would help arrive in time? He sensed an urgency to get to the scene as quickly as possible.

CHAPTER 25

Eddie and Bobby were throwing the purses in the contractor bags as fast as they could. Both kept looking up, making sure none of the women tried to escape. They had figured they would be in the church no longer than four to five minutes. These old ladies with their many infirmities would probably be so scared and traumatized that they would get confused and flustered when trying to describe them to the police and, therefore, wouldn't be credible. Eddie and Bobby wore no disguises but did wear baseball caps, hoping the bill of the cap would shade their faces somewhat.

The room was perfectly quiet, for Eddie had told them to keep their mouths shut and no one would get hurt. Eddie and Bobby didn't want the ladies to be able to recognize their voices either, so they tried to say the minimum things necessary. Besides, Eddie knew if they talked, they might forget and call out the other's real name.

Just as they were about to close up the last contractor bag of purses, they heard a siren and glanced at one another. Hopefully, it was an ambulance or fire truck passing by, but the sound cut off abruptly and Eddie's heart began to pound. He didn't like the sound of that. There was no way the police could be here. How would they have known there was a problem at the church?

Bobby moved to the back of the sanctuary and glanced through a foyer window. Two deputies were getting out of a sheriff's car slowly. Their eyes were perusing the parking lot as they were making their way to the church doors in the front. Eddie could tell by the scared look on Bobby's face that the police were here, even before he spoke.

"It's them," Bobby said.

The women started to whisper, and Eddie immediately pointed the gun at them and quietly directed them to shut up. Silence became immediate.

"Meg Foster. Step forward now!"

Eddie whispered to Bobby and quickly initiated the only plan they could.

"Organist, get up here and play a hymn. You women start singing to the top of your lungs."

Bobby aimed a gun at Meg Foster, and with his left hand took her arm and firmly escorted her out of the sanctuary and down the hallway. He figured the police would try to enter the side door to come to the office since they couldn't get in through the front doors. Perhaps they would call into the office. They needed Meg to convince the deputies that there were no problems whatsoever.

"We need to darken these windows. How can we do that?" Bobby asked, keeping the gun pointed at her.

"We have some construction paper left from vacation Bible school in one of the classrooms. We can tape it over the windows," said Megan in an almost inaudible whisper from total fear.

Just then they heard the police trying the door. It was locked from the inside. The sunlight was so bright that one officer put his face almost on the window, putting his hands around the sides of his face, trying to deflect the blinding reflection of the sun and see inside the hallway.

"Talk to him through the door, Meg. Convince him you are all right, or there will be fifty dead women in the next five minutes."

Meg stepped in front of the glass door.

"Yes, officers? Is there a problem?"

"We thought maybe you were having one," said one deputy. "May we step inside and speak to you, please?"

"Well, actually, our janitor locks the doors from the inside when our Bible study ladies are in the sanctuary and our pastor is gone. He does it for our protection. I don't have access to the key, but I assure you we are fine," Meg said as convincingly as she could.

"We had a report that there were two gunmen stealing purses inside. Locking the doors from the inside is a violation of the law. Should people need to escape a building because of a fire or whatever reason, they couldn't do that. Can you get the janitor to unlock these doors please so that we may come in and look around?"

"Our custodian had to leave to run an errand, and I'm not sure when he's coming back. I will make sure he unlocks the doors from the inside and never does that again. But officer, our ladies are singing in the sanctuary and are just fine." Megan rolled her eyes at the two policemen, hoping they would pick up on her body language. The gunman whose name she didn't know was standing at an angle and couldn't see her give the deputies a sign that things weren't right and that they, indeed, were in need of help.

The officer did pick up on it, she could tell. He nodded, gave her a wink, and as he looked at his partner, he said, "Okay, ma'am. We're glad everything is okay, but make sure the custodian knows he can't lock those doors from the inside. If we come back another time and find this, the church will get cited. By the way, what is your name?"

"Megan Foster. I'm the church secretary for Pastor Greg Myer. Thanks for your concern, officers," she answered sweetly.

The officers turned and headed toward their squad car.

"Step away from the door, Meg," Bobby said. "Let's go get that construction paper and cover the windows and doors."

Meanwhile the ladies were singing

Be not dismayed what-e'er betide,
God will take care of you.
Beneath His wings of love abide,
God will take care of you.

God will take care of you,
Through every day, O'er all the way.
He will take care of you,
God will take care of you.

When Bobby and Meg returned to the room, Bobby whispered to Eddie, "The police came to the door and Meg spoke to them. They saw the doors were locked from the inside. She gave an explanation why that was, but I'm not sure if they bought in to it or not. She tried to assure them everyone was fine, but I'm not sure they're convinced. Let's see if they drive away. We need to get out of here, and now!"

The deputies returned to their car. One got on his radio while the other deputy stood on the passenger's side studying the building and gandering at the parking lot.

Both men knew this problem wasn't over. They would try to wait this out, or they might have to move to plan B. How could the police have known and so quickly? Time to get an answer. There had to be a snitch in the room, and Eddie was determined to find her. One of these heifers had no idea what a bad mistake she had made, but if their plan was foiled, she would know very soon.

CHAPTER 26

The officer made a call into the station and reported to his superior officer, Sid Portman.

"I think we have a situation, sir, at Gospel Bible Church. We weren't able to enter the church despite a ladies' Bible study going on inside. All of the doors to the building are locked from the inside. There are at least forty cars in the parking lot, so we know there are quite a few women in there. We were able to speak to the church secretary—a Meg Foster—through a locked side door. She indicated everything was fine but rolled her eyes to indicate something was wrong. She also looked scared. Officer Dann and I sense there is someone inside who is creating a problem. We walked around the building and couldn't see anyone through the doors or windows. What do you want us to do, sir?"

"We're going to send some backup. Stay right there. If the text that was sent to a detective from her mother that two men are inside stealing their purses, we may have a hostage situation on our hands. Stay alert. We're going to call into the church and see if we can make contact. Meanwhile, we need to get hold of the pastor."

"All we know," said Officer Mike Walsh, "is that she said the pastor wasn't in the building. She didn't say where he was. We sensed someone was very close by controlling what she said. Something is stinking, boss."

"We'll get back to you in a few minutes. Meanwhile, get the license plate numbers of every vehicle in that parking lot just in case we need to determine the names of those who may be in that building. It may lead us to the suspect or suspects."

"Roger, sir."

CHAPTER 27

Sergeant Portman googled the church and found the pastor's name, Greg Myer. Once he had his name, address, and home phone, he was able to look further and learn the name of Pastor Myer's wife. The sergeant called the home phone number, but there was no answer. He then left a generic message for either of them to call his office ASAP and provided his office phone number.

Sergeant Portman also made a call into the church to see if anyone would pick up the phone. There was no answer and no answering machine came on, which was odd for even a church to miss opportunities for business if the receptionist had to step away from her desk for a period of time. While he himself never attended that church before, he had heard it was a pretty active and charitable organization even though it was a rather small one. It was highly respected in the community.

He made a quick analysis of the situation with little known facts—only assertions at this point. If someone did enter the church to steal purses, they hadn't set their standards very high. It probably would take at least two thugs to control the number of women there. They hadn't attempted to rob a bank, so maybe the suspects were quite young. And if they were young, they would most likely be inexperienced, and if they were inexperienced, we should be able to get control of the situation without anyone getting hurt. However, young, inexperienced kids can freak out, panic, and it could have a bad ending, so he didn't want to underestimate the situation either.

How many people go to church carrying boat loads of cash on them? Since they were picking on a ladies' Bible study, they knew they wouldn't be contending with men, so they chose a group that would most likely be subservient and surrender their possessions without a fight. Since most of the ladies are homemakers or retired women, they would rather give up their purses than their lives. Was this church targeted for a particular reason? Could this be more than a robbery? Just what was going on here?

Sergeant Portman then googled Megan Foster and got an address and phone number for her. He tried her home and got hold of Jenelle Musselman, Meg Foster's mother. According to Mrs. Musselman, she babysits Megan's five-month-old baby girl every day Monday through Friday. Megan calls her at lunchtime to see how things are going. Mrs. Musselman hadn't heard from Megan today, however, which she confessed was highly unusual. She gave Sergeant Portman Megan's cell phone number.

Mrs. Musselman was more than a little curious as to why the sergeant was trying to call Megan. He tried to allay her fears and arrest her curiosity, but he needed to find out more about the church and the ladies' Bible study without eliciting concern.

He learned that Mrs. Musselman and her husband have attended Gospel Bible Church for more than fifteen years. She knew that Pastor Myer had a funeral today of one of their parishioners, a mother of three by the name of June Murdoch. In fact, she had been to the Anthony and Son Funeral Home in Green the evening before for the calling hours. The funeral was at 10:00 a.m., according to the church bulletin, she thought, followed by a family dinner at Prime at Anthes on Manchester Road.

The sergeant said it was the pastor he needed to get hold of, not Megan. He also told her there was nothing to worry about at the present time, and he was guessing that Megan had just gotten tied up with the ladies' Bible study. He thanked her for the helpful information and hung up.

So this young mother hadn't called home at lunchtime to check on her baby. That more than anything raised concern for Sergeant Portman. He was beginning to sense an ugly situation brewing.

CHAPTER 28

Donna Gifford sped into the church parking lot and immediately spotted the police car. Both officers were canvassing the lot, studying every license plate number of every car. The suspicious vehicle, however, was the truck parked on the side of the building, hidden from the view of passing traffic. Mike Walsh called the plate number in. The truck was registered to a Frederick Flatt, but there was no notation of a truck or matching license plate being stolen. Chances are it would be found to be stolen, but on the other hand, many criminals are not usually cranial powers.

A police car was sent to the residence in downtown Akron, but the police found the house to be vacant and pretty much in shambles. They spoke with a neighbor who, luckily, knew Frederick Flatt.

"Yes, officer. He lived here for close to two years. He was a quiet guy. Freddie stayed to himself most of the time. He had very little company. I think he may have had a brother, but they weren't too close. I think the brother traveled around a lot."

"Do you know where we might find Freddie? Does he work?"

"No, sir. He doesn't work. Well, he might be singin' with the angels," he said as he smiled.

"The angels? You mean like the Hell's Angels?"

"No. I mean like the heavenly angels. Freddie died at least five months ago."

CHAPTER 29

Before the police left, they learned from the neighbor that Freddie died from cirrhosis of the liver at age 33. He had been a nonfunctional alcoholic ever since he moved into the hood.

When the officer checked Flatt's criminal record, he discovered he had several DUIs but no known criminal record. That certainly didn't mean he had never committed a crime. It just meant he may never have gotten caught. Records showed he was single.

The officer looked through the windows of the vacant home. It bore no furniture whatsoever. There was a Condemned sign on the front door, and it appeared the house had become the property of the city.

Well, whoever was driving that truck, for sure, wasn't Frederick Flatt.

CHAPTER 30

Donna Gifford having just arrived walked up to the two officers and identified herself as the detective who received the text from her mother about two men stealing their purses and then reported it to the police. Donna also notified them that she attended this church on Sundays and knew that her mom was inside the building, pointing to her mother's car.

She provided them with her background information. As soon as they linked her to being an employee of Doug Conrad's, they knew she was legitimate. She gave them her mother's name and then asked them if they had been able to enter the church.

"No. It's locked from the inside. It looks like some kind of power locks used for bikes."

They were telling her about their brief conversation with Meg Foster when Doug Conrad pulled into the church parking lot.

The young officers were thrilled to meet Doug Conrad. He had become quite an admired icon since the murder of his wife, Cynthia. It was a terrible tragedy that had played out nationally, and the entire world mourned for Doug and his family over his terrible loss. They then realized who Donna Gifford was. She was the one who brought Quinton Reed down, taking the difficult shot that the SWAT team was unable to take. They realized they were in the midst of two very experienced officers of the law.

Doug walked straight up to Donna and the detectives and got updated on the known intel. Still no word from the inside.

Donna feared for her mother's life. If these men were holed up in the church with weapons and they were now aware of the police presence outside, they were now holding these women hostages and negotiations needed to begin quickly before things escalated rapidly.

Officer Dann's phone went off, and he was informed of Freddie Flatt's status regarding the truck ownership. The truck had not been transferred in any other name. The truck was either stolen after the man died or is being driven by a family member. He was also told that the SWAT team would be there in minutes with a bullhorn and get set up for a hostage situation. The suspects' names, if indeed there were two and they had no reason to believe there weren't, were unknown. They would try to engage a conversation with the perpetrators soon.

Donna and Doug knew the routine well. Barricades around the church would be set up. Nearby businesses would be asked to evacuate temporarily.

They all knew that the first thing that a negotiator does is to find out as much about the hostage takers. What are their motives? The hostage taker might be emotionally or mentally disturbed, even suicidal. This could conceivably be over a domestic dispute. Typically kidnappers keep their hostages in a secret location and tell authorities what to do. However, if a criminal is cornered, such as in this case, he is likely to grab a hostage to help him escape. These guys may try to trade multiple hostages for whatever specific goals they want to achieve.

Regardless of the motivation of these hostage takers, the element of negotiating remains the same: build a rapport with them and encourage them to bring this ordeal to a peaceful conclusion.

The sooner we know who these guys are and we get a profile on them—and learn their motive—the sooner we know how to negotiate with them. If they entered the church to steal purses, then obtaining money was their motive. The texter could have been wrong about that. Perhaps it was merely an impression. But, on the other hand, it could be their sole motive. At this point, they were in need of answers.

"They are probably feeling trapped by now," Donna was saying to Doug. "They may use these fifty women as their bargaining chips."

The SWAT team arrived, and they were clearly in charge as they stepped onto the church grounds. They set up their command post. While part of the team began setting up the perimeters, Commander Bates and his assistant commander, Louie Zimmer, identified the officers who made the initial call and verified the intel. Within minutes the snipers would be in their positions on nearby rooftops, and the reaction team would be in place. They recognized Doug Conrad and also Donna Gifford from the night at Doug Conrad's home. When they found out Donna was the one who had received the text, initiated the call to the police, and that her mother was one of the hostages inside, she could be useful to them. Especially did they support her presence when they learned she also attended this church and knew the layout of the building. They allowed her to stay with them, but only if she was perfectly aware they were calling the shots and didn't come unglued knowing that her mother's life could be in jeopardy. She agreed.

Crime tape was stretched around the perimeter of the church building, designating that no one outside the SWAT team was to cross over. After the team had the church surrounded and all had quickly reviewed a rough schematic of the church building, it was time for Jon Bates, head of the SWAT team to give their negotiator, Webster Thayer, the order to make their presence known with the perpetrators inside.

Webster put the bullhorn to his mouth while standing behind a vehicle.

"This is Webster Thayer. I work with the Akron Police Department and the SWAT team. We know you are holding women of the ladies' Bible study hostages. We're not sure that was your initial intent. I need a spokesperson to call me at 555-275-0525 so we can talk and see what's going on. We want this to end peacefully. So call 555-275-0525."

They noticed that all of the doors and windows that had no venetian blinds now had black construction paper over them. Visibility inside the church was zero. Unless the SWAT team knew its correct target, which they didn't, they would never fire into the building. They didn't know the motive for the situation and still had no names or faces to go along with the crime, but their potent presence could certainly terrify a less experienced criminal to give up.

They had not met Eddie Flatt yet. If he had his way, they would never know his true identity nor Bobby's. This was the last thing they had expected to have happen to them, but they had worked out a plan for this.

CHAPTER 31

Eddie and Bobby knew they couldn't use their own cell phones or the police would learn their identity. As their hearts were pounding with fear, Eddie quickly pillaged through one of the bags and grabbed a purse. Fortunately, it had a cell phone in it.

"Whose purse is this?" Eddie demanded.

There was a pause as the women studied the purse. It took a minute for the women to focus on it.

"That's mine," yelled out Ruthann Hanna.

"Stand up!" Eddie demanded again as he was pillaging her purse looking for a notepad or piece of paper.

"What is all this shit you're carrying?" asked Eddie.

Ruthann stood. Her face was white as a sheet.

"Come here now!"

She had to crawl over four ladies to get to the aisle and then walked forward with trepidation.

Eddie finally found a piece of paper and a pen in the purse and told her to write down her cell phone number. She did. Then because they couldn't remember the number the police told them to call, they ordered Ruthann to call the police at 911. The dispatcher answered before the first ring ended.

"What is your emergency please?"

Eddie grabbed the phone from her.

"Yeah, we've got a big emergency, big guy! We've got about fifty ladies that are going to die if the cops don't back away from Gospel

Bible Church. They gave us a number to call, but I didn't have time to write it down, so maybe you can give your pals this phone number.

"Here, sister," he said to Ruthann. "Give them your phone number."

He thrust the phone in the woman's hands. Ruthann recited her cell phone number to the dispatcher and Eddie grabbed it back from her.

"Didja get that?"

"Yes, we did. May I ask who I'm speaking with?"

"Get real, mister. I'll wait for a call, but remember what I said about fifty dead ladies." He then ended the call abruptly.

Minutes later, Webster Thayer's phone rang in their command vehicle. He was given the cell phone number. After he disconnected, he boarded the tactical vehicle and as he sat down at his designated station, he dialed the cell phone number given to him by the dispatcher. Webster turned to the two men in the vehicle with him, ready to record the conversation.

"Okay, fellas. The fun is about to begin."

CHAPTER 32

"Hello. This is Webster Thayer. I'm a negotiator for the Akron Police Department. I understand there's a problem inside Gospel Bible Church. How can we end this peacefully?"

"I'll tell you how. You and your men can go away so fifty ladies don't get killed. If we don't get away scot-free, they won't."

"For the sake of conversation, may I have your name or at least a name I can refer to you as?" asked Webster calmly.

"Sure. You're talkin' to John Wayne."

There was no cocky laughter from the hostage taker, but there was a sardonic tone.

"Okay, John. My friends usually call me Web for short."

Thayer paused to see if John would initiate a conversation. He didn't.

"John, I'm going to be honest with you. We can't back away. We understand you may have the lives of fifty women in your hand, but we believe we can bring today to a peaceful conclusion, but you need to let me know why you came to Gospel Bible Church today."

Eddie didn't know how to answer that so it didn't come back to bite him in the butt, so he remained silent.

"Maybe I can make things easier on you, John. We understand that two men entered the church to steal the ladies' purses. Is that what this is about? It hardly sounds like a good reason to kill fifty ladies or put your own safety in jeopardy, wouldn't you agree?"

No response.

"Are you still there, John?"

Still no response.

"Are all of the ladies okay? No one has been hurt or injured?"

"They're all fine, for now," answered Eddie.

"That's good, John. So you went in there for some easy money and planned to slip out undetected. Am I right so far?"

"Yeah."

"Okay. Well, since no one has been hurt, you're not in that deep of trouble. How about you release all of the women and then give yourselves up. No one, and you have my word, no one will get hurt today."

"You don't get it. We're not going to prison—not ever. And right now, these hostages are our bargaining chip. If we don't escape, we're prepared to blow the church up. No one escapes!"

"Is that what you really want to have happen, John?" Webster asked calmly.

"No, but it sure as hell will if you don't meet our demands."

Webster knew that hostage takers can be extremely volatile during the first hours of negotiations because of the adrenaline following the excitement of their assault and then getting trapped before they could escape.

"I'll tell you what, John. Why don't you talk this over with your friend—and by the way, what is his name?" asked Webster in a casual manner.

"Elvis," replied Eddie in his sardonic tone.

"Okay. Talk this over with Elvis. We want you to release a half or more of the women—in good faith—and we'll see what we can do to get you away from here. After all, it will be hard to keep all of those ladies under your thumb for a long period of time. A few would be more manageable. We'll work with you, John. Talk to Elvis and get back to me in a few minutes." Webster then hung up.

He turned to his men and said, "So what do you think?"

"Well, there are probably just two men inside. If we rush the church, some women could get hurt. If the motive was to steal money out of old ladies' purses, they set the bar pretty low," laughed Scott Farley.

Commander Bates called Web.

"They sound like young punks. I doubt they brought in with them the means to bomb the church. It probably is an idle threat."

"It probably is, but we can't take the chance. Let's see what he's willing to do for assurances of a way out."

CHAPTER 33

Eddie became furious as to how the cops knew they were there. Someone—someone who was very observant and quick to react—had to have called the police as soon as he and Bobby stepped inside the sanctuary. He knew it wasn't the pastor's wife or the two ladies on stage, so it was one of the women in the pews. He was determined to find out the guilty party and make an example out of her and prove to the police that they weren't pushovers.

CHAPTER 34

J on Bates was informed that Pastor Greg Myer had just arrived on the scene and is available to provide more information about the entrances to the church and anything else they might find useful to their team. He had Reverend Myers brought to him right away. As soon as Greg walked up to him, he saw the worried look on his face.

"I'm Jon Bates, commander of the SWAT team. We are going to need some information from you that may assist us. Our goal is to get your wife and everyone else out of this situation alive."

"Certainly, Commander. I'll help in any way I can. Do we know if anyone inside has been hurt?" Greg asked with apprehension.

"We don't think so, but we can't be certain of that. We don't know who these guys are—we think there are two of them. We don't think they meant to take hostages, but when their plan went awry and the police arrived before they could execute their plan—whatever it was—and make their escape, they ended up getting closed in.

"Does your church have any enemies that you know of, Reverend?"

"No," answered Greg confidently.

"Do you know of any of the female parishioners who might be inside your church today who has some enemies who might want to hurt them—such as a recently divorced woman or one who is estranged from her husband?" Bates asked with rapid succession.

"No. None," answered Greg.

"Right now, we believe two men entered the church with the sole purpose of actually stealing the women's purses and then running. That's based on a quick text message Stella LaMarre sent to her daughter from inside the church. We know she recognized one of the men and identified him as Eugene Fielder. Does that name mean anything to you?" Bates asked.

"No."

"How many women would you approximate are in there, Pastor?"

"Usually there are about forty-five to fifty women, including my wife, Sue, who teaches the Bible study, the song director, Kaitlyn Kidwell, and her sister, Amanda Armstrong, who is the organist. Both of those girls are young mothers."

"Okay, for the sake of expediting things, I hope you don't mind if I simply call you Greg?" asked Bates.

"No, that's fine."

"Tell me about the layout of your church. Can you take this paper and draw a layout of the sanctuary, which is where we think they are, and any of the doorways, room, or hallways, etc., that extend there please."

Greg took the paper and drew a quick but accurate sketch.

"Any new people come to your church who might have caught your attention recently? Maybe they came to case it?"

"Well, we have visitors almost every Sunday, Commander, but no one who has looked suspicious. We ask visitors to sign a visitor's guest book, and then if they're local, I or one of our deacons follow up with a house call to personally invite them back. But, no, no one who looked like casing the place was their intent."

CHAPTER 35

All the local television stations and some of the radio stations had swarmed to the scene demanding to be updated on the events unfolding at Gospel Bible Church. While the press was usually a nuisance for the police, they could also be useful under certain circumstances. However, right now they were of no use and kept in what the SWAT team considered the middle ring so they couldn't film their movements. Of course the SWAT team had its own PIO (public information officer) who was on site to handle the press and news yet keeping the media from getting in harm's way.

As always SWAT was using encrypted channels so that no communications of any kind could be picked up.

Because rumors can fly faster than eagles, family members of the hostages were arriving at the scene. That was to be expected. They were being held in the outer circle and were anxiously wanting to know if their loved one or loved ones were safe. It was becoming labor intensive as these people needed to be sequestered to a nearby building where they would be questioned separately about their loved one. The Akron police force was in charge of crowd control at the SWAT team's request along with redirecting traffic.

SWAT knew that any violence usually occurs in the first three hours of the situation, so the more they could learn about every person involved—age, personality, any crucial health issues—the better they could anticipate the progression of events or what might need to be done.

Already they had been able to do a voice analysis and were pretty sure John Wayne was in his midtwenties—perhaps between twenty-four and twenty-six years. Dr. Brandon White had arrived and was sitting in the back of the tactical truck near Webster Thayer. The scribes were busy recording the time of every communication between Thayer and the hostage takers on the dry boards, which extended the full length of both sides of the command vehicle.

Hopefully, this ordeal would be over in several hours, but many such crimes weren't. You never knew going in. Things could evolve when you hadn't been able to gather all the facts. Right now the perpetrators and their motive and plan were unknown.

CHAPTER 36

Eddie and Bobby sat in the two comfortable chairs on the stage with their guns pointed at the ladies. They needed to talk without being overheard.

"You women do what you do best—talk! But if anyone tries to get up or escape, we won't hesitate to shoot you. Every door has a mini U-lock on it, and we have the keys, so you aren't going to leave this place till we say you leave. Got it?"

No one made a sound as they watched him point his gun at them.

"Do you got it, ladies?" Bobby said more emphatically. "I can't hear you!"

"Yes," said the women almost chorally.

"Okay. So start yappin'."

The women turned to one another and began to share their fears and reactions to what was happening. Some were hugging each other; then some turned to talk to those sitting behind them, but chatter they did.

Eddie turned to Bobby and began to discuss the SWAT's proposition of releasing half of the ladies.

"They want us to let half of the women go and they'll see what they can do about getting us away from here," said Eddie.

Bobby shook his head back and forth. "Yeah, they'll get us out of here to take us straight to jail. No, no way, Eddie. We need some specific promises. How do we know they'll even honor the promise?"

"We don't," said Eddie. "And usually in the movies they don't. It's just a trap, so we have to outsmart them at their game."

"Okay. Let's do that. Why don't we make a small offer to see what they do with that?" Bobby proposed.

"Like what?" asked Eddie.

"Well, I'm getting hungry. How about we ask them to bring us all Big Macs from McDonald's, and then we'll let a few women go," said Bobby.

"Yeah. That's a good idea. Let's do it."

Eddie turned to the women.

"All right, girls. Shut your traps. To show you we're not such bad guys, we're going to have the police bring us all a free lunch. How does that sound? Good? Are ya all hungry? Let's see how much your city cares about you. So I need you to be quiet while I work a miracle, okay?"

Most of the women couldn't hear a word Eddie said to them as he hadn't stepped to the podium and used the microphone. However, they had gotten quiet as they strained to hear him.

Eddie dialed the number into Web. Web picked up on the first ring.

"So, John, what have you decided?"

"Okay, Web. Here's what we need. Elvis and I and the women are getting the hungries. We *all* want lunch. We need four Big Macs, fully loaded with pickles, tomatoes, cheese, the whole works. We want twenty-three premium crispy chicken classic sandwiches and a few quarter pounders with cheese along with fries, cherry berry chillers, and twenty-five McFlurry with Oreo cookies. After we eat, we'll release twenty-five ladies. How's that?" proposed Eddie, sure that was a fair deal.

"We need the twenty-five ladies freed first, John, and then we'll send in the sandwiches and drinks. We have to know you're working with us too. How's that?" asked Webster, calmly.

Eddie muted the phone and discussed it with Bobby.

"Yeah. Let's go with it, but the ladies don't leave until the food is delivered to the door and the delivery guy walks away. Chances are they'll try to shoot us or force their way in or trick us somehow."

"Okay, so let's have them deliver it to the door on the north side, and let's insist it's a female from McDonald's who brings the food up to the door so we can see her McDonald's uniform and know it's not a cop."

"Yeah, I agree," confirmed Eddie.

"Web? Are you still there?" asked Eddie.

"Yeah, John. What did you decide?"

"When the food is delivered, bring it to the north door. We want a female from McDonald's to deliver the food so there's no funny stuff. Then twenty-five ladies will come out. We'll keep our end of the bargain. But if you try to trick us in any way, we'll kill some of the women, starting with the youngest," declared Eddie.

"No need to do any such thing, John, but how would we know that the McDonald's employee would be safe? We can't endanger anyone else here. How about one of our unarmed policemen?"

"No! We'll keep our word. Now *you* listen to us. We want what we want!" screamed Eddie into the phone.

"Okay, John. Calm down. We'll do it your way. Now, it's going to take time to get the food ordered and packaged up and brought here. The closest McDonald's is at least ten to twelve minutes from here. Be patient. We'll make this happen."

"Well, you better speed it along. Elvis and I don't have all day. We want out of here. And by the way, we want double mayonnaise and lots of pickles on our sandwiches."

Well, John, why don't we skip the lunch and see what we can do about getting you and Elvis out of the building?" asked Webster.

"Bring us the food, Web. Then we'll talk about the next step."

"While we're working on the food, John, you might want to think about the twenty-five ladies you plan to free. If I can make a suggestion, how about you let the younger women go who have young children and the ladies who have more serious health issues. After all, you don't need those kinds of problems, right?"

"Just bring the food. Elvis and I will figure out which twenty-five it will be," Eddie said flatly. He wanted to wield authority and make it appear he and Bobby held the upper hand.

"If you don't live up to your part of the bargain, John, you'll make it tougher on yourself. We want this to end quickly and—"

"Don't make no threats, Web! People could get hurt in here. Bring the food and twenty-five ladies come out."

Click.

Web spoke to Commander Bates and a call was placed to the McDonald's nearest the church. Bates identified himself to the manager and explained briefly the situation. Many times a restaurant will donate the food to the cause while other times the food money has to come out of the city coffer. This time the manager, Clifford Barkley, volunteered to fill the order and claim it as a tax deduction. That expedited things for SWAT. Mr. Barkley was informed a police officer would be over to pick the food up as well as a medium-size female McDonald's shirt.

Commander Bates informed the snipers on the roof about the food delivery and the hopeful release of twenty-five of the hostages. If this exchange went smoothly, Bates had a good feeling that this ordeal could work to their good. It is always important to let the perpetrators think they have the upper hand and are in control of matters when, in reality, they only have as much control as SWAT will allow. We play with these guys for only so long and then we make our move.

Bates was about ready to implement his plan that would curtail this morning's events and turn it into history. By evening he had plans to be eating dinner with his family.

CHAPTER 37

Donna Gifford had been sitting next to Commander Bates in the SWAT tactical vehicle for quite some time. She had been a member of the SWAT team in Charlottesville, Virginia. Her mother was one of the hostages, she knew the schematic of the church, and she was the one who actually first reported this takeover. She was calm and succinct when she spoke. She had already proven quite useful to them. Bates also knew her to be quite a heroine in Doug Conrad's case. All of the above qualified her to be sitting with him at the helm, but he asked her to step out of the truck.

She did so, and they began to have a very private, intense conversation. Doug Conrad was among those watching from the middle ring. He couldn't imagine what the two were discussing, but he could see Donna shake her head and make an emphatic gesture or two, and then Bates turned away, making sure no one could attempt to read his lips.

When the lengthy private conversation was over, it was clear they both had come to some agreement. Doug imagined that Donna would be sent to the middle ring, but instead she returned to the truck with Bates and closed the door. This seemed quite irregular from everything he knew about SWAT operations. But sometimes unusual circumstances called for unique or unusual tactics. Whatever Donna's role was, Bates had to have found it useful.

Meanwhile, Doug walked around and met up with Officer Mike Walsh.

"Hey, Officer. Do we have any knowledge about who these guys are?"

"No. They say they're John Wayne and Elvis." Walsh smiled as he rolled his eyes. "We think we may have found their truck in the parking lot. It is registered to a guy named Freddie Flatt, but we've learned he's been dead for over five months, so it's probably a stolen truck. The only thing we could see inside was a note on the front seat. We won't impound until we're sure it's the perps' truck."

"Could you read the note" asked Doug.

"Part of it, but it didn't make any sense. It looked like it was from a guy named Dexter Rabone from Eastern Capitol Bank. We couldn't see much since it was folded and the rest of the words were hidden. Maybe the truck was going to be repossessed. Can't touch the truck till Bates gives the word."

"Do you recall how Rabone was spelled on that note?" asked Doug.

"It looked like R-A-B-O-N-E. Why? Does that name mean anything to you?"

"I've heard that name before—just recently, in fact—but I can't recollect where. It will come to me," said Doug.

Doug stepped away in deep thought. He really had heard that name. It was an odd name. Not easy to remember. Maybe that was the point. It isn't meant to be remembered. Had this name come across his desk recently? He seldom forgot a name and especially if it pertained to a case he was on. It would come to him. He just needed to let the name simmer in his brain for a few minutes.

Doug began pacing and looked at the press talking among themselves, hungry for any little tidbit. He decided to call in to the office and update Jean and Mitch about what was happening at Gospel Bible Church.

"Anything happening in the office, Mitch?"

"Yeah. Barnabus just called in about twenty minutes ago. His grandmother had just passed away. He was taking it hard."

"Tell Jean to get all the information about funeral arrangements. We'll send flowers and food. Find out what Barnabus needs and get back to me.

"That reminds me, Mitch. Can you go over to my desk and open a file that is titled the Mabel Bender case? Her son, Dan, hired Barnabus to help find his mom's killer. I just took over his case. It seems like I saw a Post-It note he found by his mother's phone. Can you find that and tell me what it says?"

"Hang on, Doug."

"The file should be on the left side of my desk."

"Yeah. I see it. Okay. Let's see. Oh, here it is. It just has a name on it. No message."

"What's the name?" asked Doug.

"Dexter Rabone."

CHAPTER 38

Family members of the hostages were told to go to the John S. Knight Center on East Mill Street for a briefing of the events known so far. At first family members would be sequestered and questioned about their family member to better understand the coping skills of those held hostage. Some had multiple relatives in the building. All were very upset, which was understandable. Most were quiet with worried looks on their faces. A few were crying. Not one person had a clue who the perpetrators might be or what the motive was. A nursing home representative arrived on behalf of a resident named Gracie Holstrom. The police were surprised to learn she was ninety-five years old.

Based on the interviews of these relatives, a list was made, and it appeared that forty-eight hostages were identified as being in the church during the takeover. Gracie from the nursing home made forty-nine. The pastor's wife made up the fiftieth.

Jim Rouse stood up when the crowd was given an opportunity to ask questions.

"I have a mother and two daughters in that church. My two daughters are mothers of young children." Jim started getting choked up. "They are our world. What assurances can you give us that they are going to come out alive?" he asked sincerely.

"The SWAT team is in charge of this operation. They are top-notch professionals who are experts in dealing with hostage situations. Their record has been one of great success. Usually the perpetrators are talked out of the building peacefully once they know they have no chance of escaping. They don't want to add to their charges. The team is used to making swift decisions based on their intel. The goal is always to talk the criminal out of hurting anyone or being hurt. Yes, things can go wrong, but put your trust in our guys. They want the same outcome you want, and if it means waiting it out patiently, that's what they'll do. So we ask for your patience. We know it's hard for you."

"My name is Bill Rainey. Most of the people here know my wife had several back surgeries and became dependent on painkillers afterward. She just recently got out of rehab and is fragile right now. She gets paranoid and nervous and needs certain medicines at just the right times to keep her stable and functioning. I know she wouldn't have her medicines with her. We need to get her out of there . . . and soon!" he said with great urgency and concern.

"We're hoping at least twenty-five ladies will be released within the hour, and we've suggested the perpetrators release the younger women who have children and those with medical needs. We can't say with certainty that is what will happen. A deal has been proposed—we give them something if they give us something. So now we just have to wait and see what they're going to do."

"My name is Brad Foster, and this is Megan's mom and dad and our five-month-old baby girl, Allison. Megan, I know, is so worried about our little baby, and I'm sure she is panicking by now, not knowing if she'll ever see Allison again. She's never faced anything like this before, and my guess is she won't do well with it. I'm afraid she may become hysterical. If the SWAT team storms the church, lots of people can get killed. If they don't get these guys soon, who knows what they will do to the women . . ." his voice trailed off as he was envisioning the worst scenario.

"Try not to get ahead of yourself, Mr. Foster. We feel strongly that we can get everyone out of there alive. Please put your trust in God and the vessels God is using right now to bring this ordeal to a happy and peaceful ending. I will keep you apprised of any new events that break. Meanwhile, I will turn things over to your pastor, Greg Myer."

CHAPTER 39

Eddie was getting extremely agitated over the entire situation. There was no way this simple plan should have failed. In the other scams, which were pulled off with success, only one person was involved, and yet somehow, he thought robbing fifty old ladies in a small church would go almost unnoticed until they were able to escape. They had actually gotten away with murder but not with small theft. Today's scam was supposed to be the element of surprise, but one person in this room foiled an almost perfect plan—a well-thought-through plan—and he was about to find out who it was.

Eddie approached the podium and leaned into the microphone with his gun visible but not pointed at the women sitting in the pews before him.

"Listen up, ladies. There's something I want you to know. My friend and I swept in here thinking we would pick up some fast cash and nobody would get hurt. In and out. Get it? But then one of you called the cops and created a huge problem for me and Elvis but also for all of you. The police have surrounded the building, and now we're all put in a dangerous situation. So what I'm tryin' to say is, if that one person hadn't made that call, all of you would be safe and back in your homes by now. So I need to know which one of you ladies made the call."

There was silence in the room and not one lady so much as twitched. They were processing his words and trying to figure out what his next step would be toward that person. No one wanted to even imagine what his next move would be if he did indeed find the person. Eddie's ire was increasing, and his patience with these women was over.

He looked at Sue Myer sitting on the first pew directly in front of the podium.

"Sister, you need to work on teaching these women about honesty 'cause someone in here is a liar and a coward. Judgment is about to come upon someone unless the guilty person comes forward."

Still no one moved.

Eddie jumped off the stage and grabbed Megan Foster by her long thick brunette hair and pointed the gun to her head as he pulled her to her feet. She cried out in pain and fear.

"I didn't do it. Please! Stop! I have a baby. Don't kill me. I'll—"

Just then Waneda Robinson, Stella LaMarre, and Clare Rouse stood up almost simultaneously.

"I made the call," said Waneda. "Please don't hurt Megan. It was—"

"No," said Stella LaMarre. "She's lying. I made the call when I—"

This time Stella was interrupted.

"It was me who made the call," confessed Clare.

Just then ten other ladies stood to confess that they had been the one to make the call.

Eddie couldn't believe what he was witnessing. He was angered by their insolence. If he killed someone, there would be no escape or deal made with SWAT. So far he believed they would never be able to connect him with the murders of Mabel Bender and Lois Lawrence. The most they'd have on him and Bobby was stealing some old ladies' purses. There was no intent ever to hold them hostage or kidnap them. That was the doings of the police that forced that situation. He still believed they could work out a getaway deal with SWAT in exchange for the lives of these women.

Nevertheless, while they were in this building, these women who were bargaining chips needed to know that their defiance wouldn't be tolerated. He intended to put the fear of God in them by way of a threat. He intended to have Bobby take Megan to a back area of the church and make the women believe she would be brutally attacked or raped if the squealer didn't come forward.

Just then, before Clare, Waneda, or Stella realized it, Gracie was on her feet, walking down the church aisle with the help of her walker. She was aiming straight for the man named John even though she couldn't walk straight.

"Gracie, come back here, sweetie," called out Waneda.

Clare stepped out into the aisle to get hold of Gracie and guide her back to her seat with them. Clare had picked her up this morning from Ridgewood Place and had a responsibility to see that Gracie was safe, and now she feared for Gracie's life.

Just then Eddie pointed the gun straight at Clare and demanded she immediately sit down or he'd shoot Gracie. The women in the room gasped. The ladies in the pew where Clare stood scooted over quickly so that Clare could be seated.

Gracie continued to move toward the man with the gun. Gracie's sight was so impaired the women were sure she didn't realize the man even had a gun or that it was directly pointed at her. Gracie's facial expression was one of peace. Did she not understand the circumstances? Surely she didn't.

"Please don't hurt Gracie. She's ninety-five years old and can't see nor hear well. Please. Let us get her back to her seat," Stella called out.

Gracie stopped walking and held her hand up for the women to stop talking. She was almost in front of Bobby who was standing about six feet from Eddie. A pin falling on the carpet could have been heard it was so quiet in the room.

Then, Gracie, confused as to which man she should address, began to speak.

"I'm Gracie Holstrom. Yes, I'm ninety-five years old, and I have to pee. I still have some pride, so I don't want to pee in my pants. I have to go to the bathroom and *now*, so if you won't let me, just shoot me now, boys."

"I'll help her," shouted Clare, followed by a number of women.

"Sit down, ladies. You're not going anywhere. Bobby here will get her there." Bobby looked up, a bit surprised at Eddie's assignment for him. Eddie's main job now, and he knew it, was to negotiate with SWAT and get them out of this dilemma. If anyone could do it, Eddie could. So, all right, Bobby stood beside Gracie and walked alongside her, hoping she knew where the bathroom was.

"Support Gracie, so she doesn't fall," Stella called out with a sweet, concerned tone to her voice. Bobby took hold of Gracie's elbow, for he was clueless as to how to support her.

As they turned the corner and out of view of the other women, Gracie told him he would have to be her eyes and find the bathroom, which was down the hallway.

"Could we walk a little slower, son. My ninety-five-year-old legs can't move as quickly as yours."

"I'm not your son," said Bobby defiantly, even though he knew what she meant and how she meant it. Nevertheless, he was sensitive about the term given his background.

"I know you aren't, but I wish you were," said Gracie as she kept walking slower and slower.

"No, no, you really wouldn't wish that for yourself," said Bobby.

"And why would that be?" asked Gracie deliberately.

"It's rather obvious, wouldn't you say, Grandma?"

"How?" asked Gracie, noting that he was now calling her grandma.

"Well, maybe it's because I'm a scammer, a schemer, and in general, an all-around bad guy," admitted Bobby.

"Then I'll tell *you* what I told my sons—hit the Delete button and reprogram."

"So what are your sons doing now?" asked Bobby.

"Both of my sons are dead. My oldest boy died fighting in the Vietnam War. My youngest son was a policeman killed in the line of duty. He was only thirty years old at the time." A sad look came over Gracie's face as she spoke those words.

"Do you have other children?" asked Bobby curiously.

"No. Those were my only two, so you see why I wouldn't mind having another son?" asked Gracie as if it all made perfect sense to her.

"I bet your two sons weren't bad like me," responded Bobby.

"I was very proud of my sons. They weren't perfect, but they were good boys. I needed someone to love and someone to love me, and now they're all gone."

"Where is your husband?" inquired Bobby.

"Herb was by my side for sixty-two years, loving me until the day he died." Bobby could see her envisioning her two sons and thinking about her husband. She seemed to have no fear of Bobby even though his holstered gun was visible. *The old lady probably couldn't even see it,* he thought.

"So you see," she went on, "there's really nothing you or your friend could do to instill fear in me, Elvis. Elvis, right? I've lived a long and fruitful life, and I'm ready to meet my Lord and my family," Gracie said with confidence and surety.

They got to the bathroom doorway, and Bobby opened the door and aided Gracie into the room and over to the handicap stall. He held the door open for her as she got in and turned around. She was unable to actually close the door behind her, and Bobby could see she was quite wobbly.

"Like I said, son, I have my pride still. I'm going to need you to help, but you need to turn away while I go, okay?"

"Uh, yeah, sure."

He could hear Gracie urinating and then her sighing as she was struggling to pull her panties up. Every movement for her was labored.

Bobby was partially raised by his grandmother, but she had been inattentive to his needs, totally disinterested in his life, and certainly no love had ever been extended to him. She was nothing like this old lady. Maybe if this lady had been his grandmother, things would have been different for him, he thought to himself.

"Oh," said Gracie. "I need your help to get through this narrow door."

"We need to get back. Eddie's going to need me to help." Then Bobby realized he slipped up and used Eddie's real name. Hopefully, the old lady didn't realize he had done that.

"You know, Elvis, this may be the most dramatic and exciting thing that has ever happened to me in my lifetime, but now I'm too old to write a book about it. I don't have that much time left. And, besides, by the time I collected my pen and writing tablet, I would forget most of the details." A smile came upon her face.

"I need to stop at the basin and wash my hands."

"No. We need to go," Bobby said firmly.

"Please, Elvis. I need to wash my hands. Your friend can wait. It doesn't look like any of us are going anywhere for quite some time. Your friend seems to be the feisty one, but surely you can give me another minute.

"I do hope you both come out of this unhurt, but I hope you won't hurt any of the ladies here. Could we perhaps make a deal right here, young man?" asked Gracie pensively.

"A deal? What kind of deal?" asked Bobby defensively.

"If anyone gets hurt or has to be sacrificed, I want it to be me. Do you understand? I have lived a full, rich life. God's been so good to me, and I'm ready to meet my—"

"God's been good to you? How's that? Your two sons died before their time and your husband's dead," reasoned Bobby as he interrupted her.

"Yes. How well I know that, but I thank God for every day I had with them, not for the days I didn't," she replied.

Bobby saw how her eyes sparkled as she reminisced in her mind about those days together. He had never known a lady as sweet as she was.

"So what is your real name, Elvis?" she asked.

"Bobby."

"Oh, dear. My first son's name was Bobby. Well, it was Robert Edward Holstrom, but Herb and I always called him Bobby. So you see, you could have been my son."

"I'm tellin' you, Gracie. You wouldn't want a son as bad as me. Trust me. I've been bad pretty much my whole life," confessed Bobby.

"I want you to remember two things, Bobby. How you start your life and live it is not nearly as important as how you end it. You need to finish well. That's crucial, and it can be done if you want it."

"And what's the second thing?" asked Bobby.

"I am willing to walk out of this church together with you and to ensure your safety. I promise I will help you through this pile of trouble you've gotten yourself into. Remember what I said. Hit the Delete button and reprogram."

Bobby started to cackle. If only things were that easy. This old lady was something else. He liked her.

Bobby took her arm after she dried her hands and aimed the walker for the hallway and the long walk back to the sanctuary.

"Gracie, you need to keep our first names a secret. Eddie will be mad at me if he knows I told"

"Your secret will be kept. My memory ain't so good these days anyway, so don't fret. Now don't forget my proposition to you. And, Elvis, thanks for being so respectful back there."

As they walked back into the sanctuary, the women had their heads down and were weeping quietly.

Sue Myer, the pastor's wife, looked up and spied Gracie.

"Praise God! Gracie's okay," she said audibly. Eddie noticed how attentive Bobby was to the old lady and even escorted her back to the pew she had been in.

Stella, Clare, and Waneda gave her a big hug as she sat down next to them. Waneda kissed her on the cheek. The ladies sitting in front turned around and grabbed Gracie's hand. The ladies sitting behind Gracie leaned forward and patted her on the back or shoulder. Tears, tears everywhere.

Eddie had no idea what they were crying about. An old lady goes to the bathroom, and when she comes back, they all have tears of joy? These women were downright spooky, he thought.

Now he knew what Web meant when he said it would be hard to keep all of these ladies under their thumb for a long period of time.

Geez! And he still hadn't found out who made the call. They all confessed to doing it.

CHAPTER 40

Eddie figured the food from McDonald's should be arriving soon, so he and Bobby needed to quickly choose which twenty-five women they would release. In order to maintain control, he decided not to surrender the younger women. They would serve as strong bargaining chips, but he would release some of the old biddies with health issues. If for some reason they keeled over in here, he and Bobby would get blamed for it.

Eddie stepped up on the stage once again and approached the podium. He leaned in to the microphone.

"Okay. To show the cops Elvis and me are really good guys who have no intent to hurt any of you, we're going to free twenty-five of you women. So listen up, ladies. I want all of you who have pretty serious health issues to stand up."

At first no one stood to their feet. Some of the women leaned toward their neighbor and whispered something in her ear.

Sue Myer turned around to see who was standing. Much to her surprise, no one was standing. Finally, four elderly women stood up. Three of the four were aided by canes.

"I need you ladies to go sit in the back row." None of them moved.

"What part of that didn't you get, ladies? Move!" yelled Eddie out of frustration. He could see the ladies near them were instructing them what to do. Clearly those ladies had serious hearing impairments.

"That's only four women. I need twenty-one more. Bobby, who's the granny you took to the bathroom? She goes." Then Eddie realized he had slipped up and called Elvis Bobby. Hopefully, the ladies didn't catch his slip.

Bobby was relieved that Gracie would be getting out. He walked over to Gracie and told her to get the ladies with her to assist her to the back.

Gracie conferred with Stella, Waneda, and Clare. Stella rose to assist Gracie, but Gracie crossed her arms in defiance and wouldn't move. All of Stella's prodding and her other friends' encouragement never convinced Gracie to stand up. Gracie insisted on staying with her friends.

Bobby walked over to the women.

"If you women go with her, Gracie will go."

"Gracie needs to go for sure. We three are healthy and wish to remain here with the other women."

"Come on, Gracie. I'll help you. Let's go," urged Bobby.

Gracie looked straight ahead with an obstinate posture that was easily readable.

"I'm not going, Elvis. You know I made a deal with you, and I'm as good as my word."

"Gracie, you need to go. We'll be fine," her three friends assured her.

"I'm not going, and that is final!"

Sue Myer could tell what was happening among her women. She knew them all so well. She knew their sacrificial and loving hearts. Sue also knew that twenty-five women had an opportunity to leave in safety and that needed to happen. She knew most of the health issues of her women. After all, she and Greg had made hospital calls on them when they had surgeries, and the Bible study had made many of their health problems a matter of prayer.

Worried that John may retract the offer, she turned to the ladies.

"The man said we need twenty-one more women to go." She looked directly at John and asked if she could choose the women as she knew which women had conditions that could get serious if this day turned into hours.

"Yeah. Go ahead."

"All right, ladies. When I call out your name, I want you to stand up and go sit in the back of the church as John said. Rose Barry, Bernice McCall, Lola Mae Dennison, Nell Hollinger, Frieda Rausch, Mattie

Hurst . . ." and the list went on. Finally, there were twenty-five women sitting in the back.

The phone rang, and Eddie answered it immediately.

"Okay. This is Web. The food is about to arrive—we suspect in five or ten minutes. Do you have twenty-five ladies ready to release?"

"Yes, we do. Now listen, Web. When the side door is opened to let the women out, the girl with the food better be standing close to the door. If an attempt to force your way in is made, we will hit our remote and blow the entire church to kingdom come. No one will come out alive. Do you get that?"

"I get it. Now, John, let's review this so we can have trust on both sides. Twenty-five ladies are released—hopefully, some are the young mothers."

Web waited for affirmation but to his disappointment got no response back from John. Since it was just a suggestion and he didn't want to get John's ire up in case he backed out of the deal altogether, he moved on.

"Then the McDonald's representative will drive up and leave the food ten feet from the door. Someone from inside needs to step out and bring the food in. The McDonald's female is not to be put in jeopardy whatsoever. If anything goes wrong with the exchange, all bets are off with our deal."

"Listen, carefully, Web. She will go unharmed, but she needs to bring the food closer to the door. One of the ladies being sent out will pass the food into us. After we eat, I'll give you a call. You might want to start working on a plan to get me and Elvis on a plane to the Caribbean or you'll have mass murder on your hands. We need to get out of the country."

"What—"

Click.

"Obviously Eddie really thinks SWAT is going to let them leave the country," Web said to his team who could hear the entire conversation.

"So there's nothing wrong with letting him believe just that," said Dr. Brandon White. "Make fake arrangements, and while in transport to the airport, close in. Once we make sure every woman inside is accounted for and safely out and the church building has been left intact, surround their transport."

One of the objectives of a negotiator is to prolong the situation. The longer a hostage situation lasts, the more likely it will end peacefully.

Web knew he would stall, telling John he would need to consult with an official who had more authority. He would try to push back any deadlines John would insist on, focusing the hostage takers' attention on details such as what type of airplane they wanted and asking them open-ended questions rather than yes or no questions. The twenty-five released hostages could provide invaluable information about the locations and habits of the captors, a description of each one, and identify with certainty the other hostages.

Web knew he should never argue with John nor say no to any of his demands. Instead, he should use the delay tactics or make a counteroffer. Foremost, Web needed to keep a positive and upbeat attitude, reassuring these guys that everything would work out peacefully. He also needed to seem credible to the captors by acting like he understood the reasons for their actions but still come across as strong. He needed to encourage them to get to know their hostages and to see them as human beings, for then it becomes more difficult to execute them.

Now that Commander Bates knew what the next demand was going to be, the team began to plot its own tactical steps.

Doug Conrad informed one of the police officers standing guard in the middle perimeter that he had some information that might point to who one of the hostage takers might be. The police officer got hold of Bates and passed that information on.

"Get Conrad up here right away," ordered Bates. Doug Conrad was met outside the tactical vehicle by Bates.

"What've you got, Doug?" Bates asked curiously.

"A part of a note was spotted inside the truck parked on the north side of the church. That truck is most likely—"

"Yes, we know that, Doug. Get to your point." Understandably, Bates had a lot on his mind and felt under pressure.

"The name on that note was Rabone. That name may have a possible connection to the Mabel Bender murder. That name was on a Post-It found in her kitchen. No one could tie it to anything. If that is the case, the guy inside could be Mabel Bender's murderer, and he's more dangerous than just a purse snatcher."

"Are you working on the Bender case, Doug?"

"The son hired one of my detectives to help find his mother's murderer. I'm now working the case. This was a lead given to me."

"Okay. We'll impound the truck and get that note removed. This could prove more interesting, for sure. Thanks. This could be a big break for all of us, but it increases the risks, if this tip proves to be true."

As Doug started to return to the middle circle, he saw Donna Gifford step out of the SWAT vehicle.

"Donna. Any word on your mom?" asked Doug.

"No, but these guys have demanded lunch brought in from McDonald's. Guess I'm going to be the delivery girl."

"You? Why you, Donna? Can't—"

"They are demanding a female McDonald's employee deliver it, so I'm going to be their girl."

"Are you . . . is there a plan for your safety? How are they backing you?"

"I'm just dropping the food off ten feet from the door. I won't be in any impending danger. Twenty-five ladies will be released, so it's a good deal."

Donna had an impish look on her face, but it was one of peace. He had never seen that facial expression on her before. Yes, he knew she had been a former SWAT team member in Virginia. She was competent and experienced in situations like this before, but because her mom was in that church, Donna shouldn't be involved except to help SWAT with the layout of the church and provide personality descriptions of those hostages that she knew personally. A feeling was coming over Doug. It was an uncomfortable feeling. A sixth sense was raising the hairs on the back of his neck.

"Be careful, Donna. I mean it. These guys may very well be murderers. We aren't entirely sure, yet but—"

"Trust me, Doug. I will be."

It wouldn't be long before Doug would know the meaning of that look. As he looked up, he saw a minivan pull up with food from McDonald's.

CHAPTER 41

Donna Gifford had been totally prepped by Commander Bates. She quickly put on the McDonald's blouse that the manager had supplied for her and had even made her a badge with her first name on it so that it looked really authentic and worn. Donna put her spy pen in the lapel pocket. It was a Sony product made in China. Hers was the best on the market. Unlike others found on the Internet that have flashing mode lights during recordings, hers didn't. Hers could record up to seventeen hours continually in the manual mode and months in the motion mode. When someone entered the field of view, motion would be activated and would silently record video and audio and then stop and save the recording once they leave the field of view. Donna had paid $179 for the pen and never left home without it.

Donna's mind was racing. Surely Gracie Holstrom at age 95 would be one of the ladies released. And then of course, it would only make sense for Clare, Waneda, and her mom, caregivers of Gracie, to be released as they were probably among the oldest of those fifty women. She was counting on that being the case with the release of the twenty-five women.

Now if for some reason her mom wasn't one of the ladies who came out, Donna had decided—yes, against her trained judgment—to go against the SWAT commander's orders and deliver the food into the building herself. Thermal imaging was in place, the reaction teams were ready as were the snipers. Tear gas was on the premises; equipment to breach the doors if necessary was nearby—she knew the routine from the days on SWAT in Virginia. She had enough respect to not cause a panic situation since she could use her spy pen to talk to Bates. She could not lose her mother—would not let that happen. She had lost her husband and father in the last few years, and if anything happened to her mom, she had no reason to live either. She felt confident enough she could go in there without creating havoc, and if the other ladies who knew her didn't give her career away, her job experience could go undetected, and she could provide the SWAT commander with their picture and allow them to see everything going on inside the building. Bates might be livid with her, but if everything comes out okay, he would surely get over it, and her consequences would be minimal. At any rate, it was a risk she was willing to take.

Everything was now in place, so Web was instructed to make the call to John. Meanwhile, snipers on the rooftops of nearby buildings were on high alert. No one was certain if the perpetrators were mental midgets or were two guys who were crazy like a fox.

John answered the phone but said nothing.

"Web here. The food has arrived. The lady is going to drive up in a car and drop the baskets of food on the sidewalk approximately ten feet from the north door as you have instructed. At the same time, you have twenty-five ladies walking out that door. Are we on the same page, John?

"Yeah. We're on the same page."

"Good. Meanwhile, we are searching for a way to get you to the Caribbean. We think we may have a way to get you to Saint Thomas Island, but we're still trying to work out the logistics. Let's get this first step completed. If you want to send more ladies out than the twenty-five, it would be a great gesture." Web was trying to get as many ladies out of there and to safety as possible.

"You'll get twenty-five ladies, Web. That was our deal."

The phone went dead.

"You ready to move, Donna?" asked Bates.

"Yes, Commander."

"We're getting the audio and video clearly. No heroics, but if you can get close enough without going in to get a glimpse of them, that could be the break we need in identifying them. But again, no heroics, Donna. We can get a description of the two of them from the ladies released. Good luck."

The food was in the back seat of the car, and Donna drove to the north side of the building. She was nearly beside the truck believed to be John and/or Elvis's. She paid no attention to it, however, as she needed to stay focused on her task at hand. As she opened the trunk and began unloading the baskets of food, the north door opened, and women quietly began walking out. Donna held her head down so none of the ladies would recognize her. Frantically she searched for her mom, Gracie, Clare, and Waneda. So far they had not come out. She informed the ladies that a bus was just around the corner and they would be bussed to safety from there. As the twenty-fifth lady exited, Donna's heart sank with the realization that neither her mom nor any of her friends were among the released. She was disappointed, for sure, but not really surprised. Her only surprise was that Gracie wasn't one of the twenty-five. She had to be the most qualified person on the list for release.

The last lady who exited was Vera Lonsbury. Donna quickly recognized her.

"Why, Donna, it's you. I've been instructed to carry the food in."

"Hi, Vera. The plans have changed a bit. You go on and step around the building quickly. I'll be taking the food to the door now."

"But I was told I have to—"

"Really, it's okay, Vera. Quickly. You need to get around the corner. Everything will be fine."

"Oh, God bless you, Donna," she whispered. "Your mom is in there, but she's okay."

"Good, Vera. Now go."

Donna spoke loudly enough for the spy pen to detect her voice.

"Commander, there's no way Vera could pick these baskets of food up by herself, so I'm going to take them up to the door. My mother is still in there."

Bates always worried when original plans weren't followed, but he also knew there had to be flexibility under circumstances such as these. He just hoped this wouldn't backfire on them and cause distrust on the perps' part. Somehow Bates worried that Donna wouldn't just take the food to the door, slide it in, and leave. His instincts were correct as he watched Donna walk in and shut the door behind her. Not even once did she look back.

CHAPTER 42

All twenty-five ladies sat on the bus and were driven to a nearby building where they were sequestered for questioning. At this second command post, the assistant commander had his operatives set up to interrogate each former hostage. Tactical medics were on site to assist any of the ladies who might need medical assistance. Most of the ladies were just frightened and tense but admitted that no harm had come to them.

At the end of the interrogations, the factual things they had gathered that were consistent among all twenty-five ladies was that there were only two perpetrators—both males were in their mid—to late-twenties or possibly early thirties. Both were of medium height and both carried guns. One had light brown hair, the other dark brown hair. Both wore blue jeans. Elvis had a tan T-shirt with red vertical stripes on and had been nice to Gracie. John Wayne was the scariest. He did most of the talking. He looked mean. According to many of the ladies, "He had a look in his eye."

After that, the operatives wondered how so many women could be in the same room, witness the same things, and yet see so many different things—from a red shirt to a bright yellow one. No one had seen any remarkable characteristics on them such as tattoos, scars, warts, facial hair, receding hairlines, glasses, jewelry, etc.

Not much was gleaned from the ladies that proved useful in identifying these guys. All had expressed their gratitude for being rescued safely, and all expressed their utter fear for the ladies left behind. And every one of them had admired Gracie Holstrom for her gutsy spirit.

Pooling all of their facts from the interrogations led their team to wonder one thing. Who was this Gracie Holstom?

CHAPTER 43

A gun was pointed directly at Donna's chest.

"Turn around and go back out," demanded Bobby. He tried to sound threatening and intimidating. "The deal was the last lady out was to bring in the food, not you, lady."

"That's what I was told as well, but it was too heavy for her and she couldn't lift the baskets. These are heavy, especially the ones with the beverages in them."

"So turn around and get the heck out of here," he demanded again. "We made a deal with the cops, and we need to keep it."

Donna tried to look like someone who had never had a gun pointed directly at her, but the truth of the matter was, she had, many times. It always scared her, but she felt she could talk the criminal down.

"All I know," said Donna as innocently as she could, "is that this is my church, and my mother is somewhere in here. If she would have come out, I wouldn't have dared to come in."

"Are you a cop? Put your hands up."

"No, I'm a low-paid gopher for McDonald's. Can't you smell the lousy grease on my clothes? Please don't shoot me. My dad died three years ago, and my husband died a year ago. I can't lose my mother. She's all I got. I can't leave without her. I won't leave!" stated Donna with anxiety. Since it was mostly true, she did get teary eyed. Anyone watching Donna would have agreed she earned an Oscar Award for her performance.

Donna complied quickly by putting her hands up, and Bobby patted her down. He went from her shoulders to her torso and waist and then to her crotch. He pulled out her pockets and saw that they were empty. He noticed in her lapel pocket she had the order pad and pen and that she was unarmed. Of course Donna knew that Elvis was an amateur at searching people or else he would have gone down to the ankle.

Bobby had never been assertive. Eddie was best with that. When he escorted this lady to the sanctuary, he knew Eddie was going to be furious with him. If the police thought they had broken their end of the bargain, something bad could happen to them. He directed Donna to carry some of the baskets of food and drinks into this one larger room he had found. It had round tables in it that could seat about eight people per table and it had a small kitchenette. He followed behind her carrying some baskets as well, but he continued to keep a gun pointed at her at all times.

"This is our reception hall. We have wedding receptions and socials in here," Donna remarked.

"All right. Let's head for the sanctuary. Eddie's not going to like you here one bit. If you create a problem for us, I can tell you for sure that all hell is going to break loose."

Okay, Donna thought to herself. *So John Wayne's first name is likely Eddie.* Elvis didn't even know he had said it, so her entering the scenario rattled him enough to make an important mistake. He wasn't a very experienced or professional criminal, and right there was proof. She also knew that Commander Bates and the scribes all heard the name.

As they moved into the sanctuary from the hallway, Eddie could be heard talking on the cell phone.

"She did what? Elvis wouldn't allow that."

Eddie looked up and saw Bobby following the McDonald's girl into the room with a gun pointed to her back. Eddie put the phone on mute after telling Web to hold for a minute.

"She's going to be a cop, Bobby! She's a plant!"

So, now, Donna and the team learned the other guy's name was Bobby.

Eddie didn't even know he had slipped up. That was the trouble with using aliases under circumstances like this. You get the slight bit rattled, and you revert to reality.

"No, she's not, Eddie."

Both men were panicked enough not to realize they were using each other's real first names. Still, they needed to get last names so criminal records could be checked.

"I body searched her. She has no weapons on her anywhere. I can vouch for that," he said with a confident sneer on his face.

Donna was thankful he had not taken his hands all the way down her legs or he would have surely felt her ankle holster and known she was carrying.

"She goes to this church, Eddie. Her mom is in here. That's why she volunteered to deliver the food. Her McDonald's was the one who supplied the food. That's how she found out about the church takeover."

"Who's your mom?" asked Eddie.

"Stella LaMarre," answered Donna without any hesitation.

"Stella LaMarre? Standup," yelled Eddie.

Stella saw her daughter walk in with a gun pointed to her back. She was surprised to see her daughter walk in to the room but not surprised that she had taken an active role in this situation, especially with her in here. However, she deeply regretted Donna's personal involvement but figured she was working with the authorities on a plan to get them all out of here safely. With Donna's black belt in karate, she had no doubt that Donna could disarm at least one of the criminals in seconds if given the opportunity. She also figured Donna was armed somewhere, somehow. Still, she was heartbroken Donna had interfered and was putting herself in harm's way.

Stella stood up.

"Is this your daughter?" asked Eddie.

"It is."

"What's her name?" Eddie knew she couldn't see the name on the woman's badge, so he would quickly know if this was a set up.

"Donna. She's my only child, so please don't hurt her."

Bobby decided to confirm her truthfulness by asking a question of his own.

"Is she married?"

"She was. Her husband died last year."

Bobby said, "That's the right answer, Eddie. So now what are we going to do?"

"She gets out of here now!"

"I won't go," Donna answered defiantly. "I won't leave my mother. You could release another person, and I'll stay. Maybe the cops would agree to that."

Eddie got back on the line with Web.

"Web, you better not be pulling anything on me or I swear we will kill every last living lady. Do you understand? This McDonald's chick brings the food in and demands she's staying."

"Yes, we heard. The lady who was supposed to bring the food back in to you, Vera Lonsbury, verified the story. She recognized Donna as one of the church attendees. She knew the baskets were too heavy for Vera. We didn't know the lady had her mother in the church or we would never have allowed her to bring you the food. She never said a word to us. I mean, who knew? So, now, John, either she or another lady needs to come out if we are to continue our deal. This was a kink in the road none of us expected. So what will it be? We prefer one of the younger women to come out. Some of those women are young mothers."

"All right. One is coming out. Keep working on our way out of the country. Gotta go. Our food's getting cold."

Eddie pointed a gun to the two sisters sitting in the front row.

"One of you girls are leaving. So which one?"

Kaitlyn looked at her baby sister and said, "You go, Amanda."

"No, you go, Kaitlyn. I only have one child and you have two."

"Listen, whoever stays is going to come out of this alive, so as your older sister, I'm telling you to go," insisted Kaitlyn, not really sure she was speaking the truth.

"If one of you don't leave, I'm going to shoot both of you!" shouted Eddie in total exasperation.

With tears streaming down her face, Amanda stood up, hugged her sister quickly, and followed Bobby to the hallway door. She turned and looked back at Kaitlyn and the other ladies and blew them a kiss.

"Sweet Jesus!" could be heard throughout the room. Many women were relieved beyond words that at least one young mother was freed. Kaitlyn was sobbing, and Sue Myer, the pastor's wife, had her arms around her, consoling her.

"We're moving to the room with food. Two or three of you ladies set up the food and beverages. Remember, Elvis and I get the Big Macs, and you ladies get the chicken sandwiches. Free lunch, ladies, so stop whimpering!"

CHAPTER 44

U nder police protection and the rooftop snipers, the guy from Jeff's Towing was pulling the truck off the church property. A search warrant had been rendered and perhaps more information could be obtained from within it that would put light on who these guys were. Hopefully, they had a previous record and would be in their database.

If Doug Conrad's information from the Mabel Bender case was connected to these two guys, they would better know the type of criminal they were dealing with. It certainly would help them know how to continue with this hostage crisis and how volatile it could become.

One thing was certain: twenty-five women's lives were in jeopardy here, and their SWAT team would be held responsible for getting all of them out alive.

As Bates looked up, a young woman stepped out of the church door and began running.

CHAPTER 45

Olivia Rainey and Addie Bartow stepped forward to help Sue Myer separate the sandwiches. There were Big Macs, crispy chicken classics, and some quarter pounders. There were also fries, cherry berry chillers, and Oreo cookies to organize and spread out on the tables.

The two men were standing near the doorway so none of the women could leave the room. They were whispering about what their next move would be if the police didn't come through with a flight to the Caribbean. The next phase was the tricky phase. Eddie wasn't sure if he was going to have to start hurting some of the women to prove the urgency so that the police would comply to their demands or face society's scorn when these beloved women were hurt or snuffed out. Both knew that if they killed these women, the building would be rushed by SWAT and they would either be killed or captured. Neither had any appeal to them. The plan was for each one of them to take a hostage as insurance for getting to the airport and on the plane safely. The men were engrossed in their own thoughts and planning as the women stirred around the room. Some took seats at the tables. Clare and Waneda helped Gracie to her seat and placed her walker in the corner out of the way.

Donna turned her body away from the men so there was no chance of their reading her lips. She asked her mom softly where her cell phone was.

"It's inside my blouse and has slid down to my waist."

Her mom was also wearing a quilted vest that had a tight ribbing over the blouse and hung over her belted slacks. Elthie Donovan and Millie Elkins stood in front of their table when Loretta Chapman joined them, so there was good blockage, which gave them time to make the exchange.

"Pass your phone over to me under the table. I might be able to get a quick text off."

Her mother passed the phone over, and Donna saw that the noise factor in the room was rising, making it ideal to send a message off now. Since the men were in a serious conversation—no doubt trying to figure out how to get out of this mess—this was the time to text Bates a message.

2 wht. men Eddie and Bobby Rueg + .22 C no bmbs. DG

Send.

CHAPTER 46

As the women were migrating to the church's reception room, Waneda Robinson and Clare Rouse were walking on each side of Gracie to help her navigate with her walker. As they went through the sanctuary doorway to the hall leading to the dining area, they passed the one guy who went by the name of Elvis.

Waneda's eyes met his, and he was watching her as she went by for any sign of recollection. Waneda pretended to not recognize him and looked nonchalant like she was staying focused on Gracie. After they were much further down the hallway, Waneda whispered to Clare,

"That is definitely the guy who came to my house wanting me to hire him to do yard work or any heavy work inside or out that needed to be done. He said his name was Eugene Fielder. Don't you remember me telling you about him, Clare?"

"Yes, I do. Are you absolutely sure that's him?"

"Yes. I'm certain. His voice is a match as well."

"I thought you were making a mistake not to let him help you, Waneda. I guess I was wrong. But why did he target you?"

"He said he passed by Robinson Avenue and saw me working hard in the yard and thought I could use some help."

"But how did he know you didn't have a husband who could help you?"

"Well, I guess he didn't really know that although he said he had passed my house for years going to work. He said he was out of work and hadn't been able to find a job. He had a wife and a young baby to support and could use the money."

"So he may have known you lived alone?"

"I don't know. I remember him saying he didn't have a phone when I told him I might call him later. He said he would stop by at a later day and check up on me. He just wasn't coming forward with facts about himself—like exactly where he had worked. He was too evasive."

"So your woman's intuition told you that he might not be on the up-and-up?"

"Yes. That's precisely what it was. I sensed something about him that just didn't feel right."

"So how did he end up here at *your* church? Is this a coincidence or has he been stalking you?"

That had never even occurred to Waneda, and yet, the coincidence of his robbing her church when she was there seemed to defy coincidence. A troubled look came over Waneda as she considered that as a viable possibility.

"I think I would know if someone were stalking me," Waneda said but with doubt in her voice as she tried to process that idea.

"Surely I would know that. I try to be aware of my surroundings. I know I should be observant."

"The guy is carrying a gun, Waneda. Your intuition about this guy was obviously right. If he had made his way in to your house, it is scary to think what might have happened to you. Old people are victims of scams all the time. Why, there have been several old people murdered just lately, and according to the news, they may have been victims of scams. They were vulnerable and innocent. I think you had a guardian angel watching over you, Waneda."

"I think you're right, Clare."

"The Bible says, 'It is of the Lord's mercies that we are not consumed because his compassions fail not. They are new every morning; great is thy faithfulness.'"

"Just as He was merciful to me that day, I hope He will be merciful to all of us today. I hope and pray I didn't lead these gunmen here today."

CHAPTER 47

Sue Myer noticed Olivia reaching for the Big Mac sandwiches. Very subtly she unraveled the wrap of one, reached into her pants pocket and had something in her hand, but Sue couldn't see what it was.

Olivia looked up and saw that Sue was watching.

"What're you doing, Olivia?"

Olivia raised her eyebrows, pushed her lips out as though saying "Shhh!" Olivia lifted the top of the bun off the one sandwich and slipped what looked like two capsules under a pickle slice.

"Olivia!" said Sue softly. "What is it? Could that kill someone?"

"No. It's for insomnia." She smiled. "It works better than a lullaby," she whispered.

Sue didn't have sympathy for these two guys, but she didn't want anyone to die, not even these two men. But she certainly hoped that if they did die, it was not by the hands of the ladies in Bible study.

Olivia regretted she only had two capsules. If she had had four, this ordeal would easily come to a happy conclusion in several hours. At least she was pretty sure of that. Sue was hoping Olivia could be trusted.

Olivia Rainey had been a faithful member of this church years before even she and Greg came to minister at the church. Olivia and Bill were usually the first ones to arrive at the church for any service or event and usually one of the very last ones to leave.

When Olivia had fallen down her basement stairs over a year ago, doctors weren't sure she would survive. She suffered a blood clot on the brain and had broken her back. She remained in Akron General Medical Center's ICU for almost a month fighting for her life. Bill didn't leave her side for weeks until the doctors began to offer hope. Then when she survived two surgeries and doctors assured him she was out of imminent danger, Bill went home but only at night. She remained in the hospital for weeks after that and was finally transferred to a rehabilitation facility for extensive therapy until she could walk on her own.

However, Olivia was in so much pain that she was under the care of a pain management physician. After she was sent home to wait out the remainder of a long recovery, she had trouble functioning at home without pain medication. Not long after, it was discovered Olivia was too dependent on the prescription painkillers and had created another problem for herself. She and Greg had visited Olivia in rehab at least twice for her drug addiction. Sue thought the last visit to rehab had weaned her of her addiction to the prescription drugs. Now she wasn't so sure.

The irony of all of this is that Olivia's problem could be what saves the lives of twenty-five women. *After all,* thought Sue, *God works in mysterious ways.*

CHAPTER 48

"Today was not a day like any other at Gospel Bible Church in Akron. We have an ongoing hostage situation that began this morning around eleven o'clock.

"A ladies' Bible study of fifty ladies was interrupted by two gunmen. From what authorities have said, it appears their motive was to rob the church and steal their purses. However, before they could make their escape, the police arrived, which they believe, forced the hostage crisis. The SWAT team, we are told, is at the site and has their command post set up.

"The identity of these two men is unknown, but the perpetrators agreed to free twenty-five of the fifty women in exchange for meals from McDonald's. We do know that meals from McDonald's were donated by a franchise nearby and that twenty-five ladies were released unharmed. However, twenty-five ladies still remain inside the church, and we know that the men are armed and have promised to bomb the church if they are not given a clear passage out. SWAT Commander Bates will not comment on the deal in progress or even if there is such a deal.

"The released women described the two men as white, having brown hair, of medium height, in their mid—to late-twenties. Both are wearing blue jeans and one is wearing a tan shirt with red vertical stripes. Their names may be Eddie and Bobby.

"Anyone who recognizes these descriptions or may know who these two men are should call the Akron police immediately."

Lee Jordan of Channel 5 News asked reporter Charlotte Walton at the scene, "Charlotte, do they know if these men live around here or have some relationship to the church?"

"No. None of the ladies recognized either man as a parishioner. We do know, Lee, that a black Ford truck sitting in the parking lot has been impounded and is believed to belong to the men. Perhaps more will be learned from that search, but we just don't know yet.

"The families of these women are anxiously waiting at the John S. Knight Center for briefings and updates of any progress being made.

"Pastor Greg Myer whose wife is also in that building is actually with me here. In fact, Sue, his wife, was leading the Bible study at the time of this incident.

"Pastor Myer, do we know the names of all of the hostages at this time?"

Greg Myer leaned into the mic that Charlotte was holding in front of him.

"Yes, actually we do. Most of these ladies attend Bible study every week. My wife and secretary, Meg Foster, are still in there."

"Do you feel comfortable that this will have a happy outcome?" Charlotte asked with compassion.

"We're certainly praying to that end. Family and friends of each one of these ladies have been gathered in a room here at the John S. Knight Center praying for them. We know God is with them and He's watching over them."

"So can you tell us anything about some of the hostages, Pastor?"

"Well, I know we have a few young mothers in there and that the oldest person is ninety-five years old. And, of course, everyone in between."

"Ninety-five years old? Wow! Are you worried for her?"

"Of course. I'm concerned for everyone in there. Gracie Holstrom is—"

"Is that the ninety-five-year-old woman?"

"Yes. Gracie is a remarkably strong woman in her faith. She loves everybody and everybody loves Gracie. Physically, she's frail, but God will watch over her, and I know the ladies of the church will do everything in their power to protect her."

"Well, Lee, we will be staying right here keeping you informed as things develop, no matter how long it takes. This is Charlotte Walton coming to you live from Gospel Bible Church in downtown Akron."

"Thanks, Charlotte."

CHAPTER 49

Chris Lambert was preparing dinner for her family. She had her twenty-six-inch LG TV on that was mounted to the wall in the corner of her kitchen listening to Live on Five when Breaking News came on telling about the hostage situation at Gospel Bible Church.

She listened as the hostage takers were being described. A tan shirt with red vertical stripes. Something was triggered in her mind. She had seen a shirt like that before. Had she almost bought one like that at Kohl's for her husband?

As she listened to the news story, she was hoping for a good outcome. That would be terrible if anything happened to those ladies, especially that ninety-five-year-old lady. She probably figured if she had beat death for ninety-five years, she would one day simply die peacefully. And if you're not safe in church, where could you possibly go to be safe? Old people were so vulnerable. Just like poor Mrs. Lawrence next door.

CHAPTER 50

O livia had slipped two 30 milligram Restoril capsules under the pickle of one Big Mac. One of the men would surely ingest it since they ordered only themselves the Big Mac. Olivia and Sue were hoping that Eddie, the guy who called himself John Wayne, would be the one to eat that sandwich since he seemed to be their biggest threat. He was getting more and more agitated as the day was wearing on, and he knew there was no way out of this building without fighting their way out or surrendering, which they didn't seem likely to do, or working out a deal with the authorities, which seemed even less likely.

Olivia hoped she hadn't made a mistake by putting the drug in the sandwich. If they got caught, it could easily backfire, and someone could get killed. If only she could have drugged both men, their worries would be over. They would have been no threat to anyone.

She had been prescribed the drug by her doctor for severe insomnia. According to Dr. Jacobus, Temazepam, which is the generic name for Restoril, is used by the US Air Force to help aviators and special duty personnel sleep in support of mission readiness, so she was assured it would work for her. Giving someone two 30 milligrams was 100 percent more than a normal dose, but it wouldn't be a lethal dose. Within thirty minutes, she would know which guy ingested the hypnotic, for he would be experiencing dizziness, fatigue, poor balance, a longer reaction time to things, slurred speech, flat emotions, reduced alertness, blurred vision, muscle weakness, and put him in a deep sleep for at least eight hours. Oral administration results in rapid absorption with significant blood levels achieved in less than thirty minutes, but she knew he would be completely snowed within two to three hours.

Restoril is also known as King Kong pills, terminators, wobbly eggs, and knockouts on the street, her doctor laughingly once told her. Of course she only told her that to assure her that she would be getting a great night's sleep when taking Restoril.

Olivia and Sue were the only two who knew about the loaded sandwich, and both watched the sandwiches closely, making sure none of the ladies got hold of that sandwich by mistake.

As the day was marching on, Sue could see the ladies had had enough of this drama as well and wanted to go home. Being held at gunpoint was wearing on their nerves. Megan Foster, especially, was looking quite nervous and afraid. This young mother desperately needed to get home to her five-month-old baby. The idea of not making it out alive was a possibility, but up to now, no one sensed it would actually come to that except for perhaps Megan. Ruthann Hanna was staying close to Megan, and Sue was sure Ruthann was trying to give her encouragement and assurance that this day would end well. Ruthann was a calm, laidback kind of person with an amazing upbeat and positive attitude. She would be good for Megan.

Everyone was seated at the tables. Most were already eating sandwiches, fries, and slurping on their cherry berry chillers, but there were some too upset to eat.

Eddie and Bobby walked over to the table and nonchalantly picked up the biggest sandwiches. They were obviously the Big Macs among the nine or ten sandwiches left on the table. They grabbed two fries each, several chillers, and cookies and sat in two chairs by the only door to the room. As long as they were positioned there, nobody was going to make a run for it.

Gracie was sitting at a table with Stella, Donna, Waneda, Clare, Kaitlyn, and Fannie Furman. She seemed to have a rapacious appetite although she had such few teeth in her mouth. She was struggling a bit to get the meat chewed. It seemed like Gracie was taking advantage of some good food. Donna wondered what kind of food Gracie would be eating back at her nursing home. She also seemed to be enjoying the extended time with all of her friends, not that she was glad they were all being subjected to these two gun-wielding thugs. It must be a very lonely life for Gracie, but she seemed to be at perfect peace with the situation she found herself in. Certainly Megan and Kaitlyn viewed it differently from their perspective and stage in life. Of course, that would make all of the difference, wouldn't it?

Donna was thinking that if these two men separated and were in two different rooms and if she could get at arm's reach of them one at a time, she was sure she could use a quiet and swift karate kick to disarm them.

These guys had no idea they were being seen or recorded. With this kind of red-handed evidence, these guys wouldn't have a defense in court. Donna needed some kind of a break. Little did she know that it was about to happen very soon.

CHAPTER 51

B obby grabbed the Big Mac with the Restoril in it. Olivia and Sue were so hoping it would go to Eddie, the rougher of the two guys. He seemed to be far more dangerous than Bobby.

Each man had taken two Big Macs and was talking while unraveling their first sandwich. Bobby would be eating the loaded sandwich first. Both Sue and Olivia were afraid they would check out their sandwich before eating it and discover the ruse, but both men continued talking and snarfing down their sandwich in caveman style.

Sue and Olivia tried to gaze around the room as they and the men were eating. They didn't want to be caught focusing on them in case it caused them to get suspicious. Olivia nudged Sue under the table as they watched Bobby chewing kind of funny. He kind of choked or coughed. The women couldn't tell which. They held their breath. Eddie continued to talk while Bobby lifted the top bun off his sandwich for an inspection. He looked at the beef and then lifted up the pickle.

"Oh, my goodness," Olivia whispered in a panic. "I think he's on to something."

Sue's curiosity got the best of her. She couldn't take her eyes off Bobby.

Apparently things looked okay to Bobby, and he continued to eat his sandwich while listening to Eddie.

Now Olivia and Sue knew that it must have been swallowed so that in a short while their perpetrators would be down to one. There was no chance of rushing Eddie to try to overcome him. After all, he had a gun and they didn't have one, but both ladies were sure Donna

Gifford came in to the church with a plan and fully prepared to do something. Thankfully, none of the ladies had given Donna's identity away or revealed her professional background. Surprisingly, these men didn't know who Donna was after all the publicity revolving around the famous Conrad murder case right here in Akron not more than a year ago. She certainly came with great credentials, but still, no one wanted to see bloodshed in the church.

Sue needed to speak to Donna to tell her about the Restoril. Maybe she or they could come up with a plan. These two men had no idea who they were fooling with. After all, we are soldiers of the cross!

CHAPTER 52

D oug Conrad was standing at the middle perimeter, staring at the church. Donna Gifford had pretty much invited herself into a dangerous setting, and that troubled him immensely. Over the months she had become an important person to him. In fact, she had become much more than a respected employee.

First, they both shared the loneliness of widowhood, especially at a young age. Well, rather young, anyway. Her marriage to Pete had been a long and happy one until pancreatic cancer had taken him away from her. She fought the daily battles with him for ten months, knowing that no matter how hard they fought, short of a miracle, they would lose. She felt Pete's pain and suffering. It was a journey she had wished she had not had to travel, but she did. The beautiful memories with Pete would last a lifetime, but so were the feelings of hopelessness and loss when they both realized their time together was coming to a swift conclusion. She hung on to every last intimate exchange they had with each other until he succumbed in her arms.

There were similarities with him and Cynthia. He had only six days of not knowing who had kidnapped her or why. He was emotionally tortured as he imagined what she might be going through. It was unbearable. He also knew that she had been an innocent victim because of someone who sought revenge against him. And he knew the chances of ever seeing her alive again were slim. He didn't have the privilege of last-minute intimate exchanges with her, so the lingering memories would always be fresh and poignant, and yet, he too had precious memories with Cynthia that would prevail forever. No one could take that away from him.

He recalled the day Donna walked into his business for the interview. Then, some months later, she ended up killing Cynthia's murderer and saving his and his daughter's life as well. That day it gave her a prominent place in his heart, for she ended the nightmare once and for all for the Conrad family.

Oh, yes, the job interview. This woman had totally disarmed him in her job interview by flipping him over her shoulder. And then, on top of all of that, her dog—named Chunx—pins him to the floor and then slobbers all over him. It was a French mastiff and was so strong and powerful—and overwhelming—he couldn't remember a time he had been more afraid except, of course, when his family had been threatened. He wondered what impression she had of him. He hadn't exactly looked suave on either occasion.

Donna was a compassionate person. She was able to empathize with people. He recalled how she physically held on to Wendy Graves the day her fiancé, Andy Chandler, died. She was always willing to cover for Barnabus Johnson so that he could leave work early to spend a few extra hours with his dying grandmother. According to Jean, she had done many nice favors for Mitch too. Donna didn't have an egotistical air about her in any way although she had reached every benchmark in her life and had acquired quite a few badges of courage along the way.

Probably, above all, Doug admired her loyalty to her husband, and now, here she was possibly jeopardizing her safety for her mother. He knew that was why she walked into that church with two armed men. She went in there to save and protect her mother and her mother's dearest friends or go down with them. She was totally devoted to her mother. He knew she wasn't trying to be heroic or gain public accolades from anyone. She had certainly gotten plenty of that in the newspaper over his case. Her mother was the only one left in her immediate family. Life wouldn't be worth living if her mother was gone. Doug could definitely relate to that. What would he do if he lost Paul or Taylor?

If anything happened to Donna, it would be a huge psychological setback for him. It wasn't that he had romantic feelings toward her; it's just that he had *special* feelings for her in respect to her important role in his family's problem. He had built up such deep respect and admiration for her. Like Cynthia, she was a class act and a person of true quality.

Doug knew he was in a good place in life. He was surrounded by his good partner, Mitch Neubauer; he had a very caring, loyal, and efficient secretary, Jean, who had worked for him since he started the business. He had Barnabus who had proven to be a hard worker and a tremendous asset to their cases, especially Andy Chandler's case. And then of course, Donna Gifford. All people of great character and trustworthiness.

His business was thriving, and he had all of them to thank for that as well.

And then there was his dearest buddy, Pastor Jim Pascoe and his wife, Holly, who was his support system through the ordeal with Cynthia and beyond. God brought all of these people in to his life, and he didn't want to lose any one of them.

Just then his cell phone rang. When he saw who the caller was, he lit up.

CHAPTER 53

"Hi, Dad."

"Hi, Taylor. How's my baby girl?"

There was a long pause. At first Doug thought they had a bad connection, but he could hear some indistinguishable sound.

"Taylor, are you all right, honey?"

"Yes, I'm fine, Dad. I was checking on you."

She sounded sad. He knew her well enough to know something wasn't quite right. If he kept her talking long enough, he figured she would open up.

"How are your classes going?"

"Good. I have to make a presentation in one of my classes today. I'm a little nervous, but I'm ready."

"Oh? What's the topic on?"

"It's for my psychology class. We were assigned specific topics, and mine was fate versus predestination, so I will be talking about whether things happen by blind chance or whether they are foreordained by divine decree or influence."

"That's a deep topic. Do you have to merely explain the differences or debate them and argue a position?"

"Well, I have to explain their differences, of course, but then I have to explain my position and why."

"Were you given a time limit for this presentation?"

All the while Doug was talking to Taylor, he was keeping his eye on the church and observing any movement by SWAT.

"It can't be longer than ten minutes."

"I'm sure you will do fine, honey. I have no doubt what position you will be taking."

"So, Dad, are you in your office right now?"

"No. Actually I'm downtown. There's a hostage situation at Gospel Bible Church."

"Really? What's that all about?"

Doug chose not to share more information with Taylor right then. It was almost the year anniversary of her mother's death, and he wanted to keep her mind off kidnappings. It would only stress her out if she knew Donna Gifford was one of the women being held hostage. After Donna had killed Cynthia's murderer, Quinton Reed, Taylor seemed to connect with Donna in a very special way. He didn't want this to alarm her or distract her from focusing on her classes. After all, he was pretty sure Donna and the other women were going to come out of this okay.

"We're really not sure yet, sweetie, but I think it's going to work out all right."

"Okay. Well, that's good."

"Are you coming home this weekend?" Doug asked in an attempt to change the subject. Taylor lived off campus with two of her girlfriends in an apartment, but usually if she didn't need to go to the campus library at KSU, she came home. She averaged two out of four weekends at home.

"I don't think so, Dad." There was a very long pause.

"Dad?"

"Yes, Taylor?"

"Are you sure you're okay?" she asked sincerely.

"I'm fine, honey." Now Doug was starting to understand her motive for calling.

She knew that the one year anniversary of her mother's death was in a few days, and she worried that he was feeling depressed.

"I miss your mom, Taylor. I think I know where you're going with this. Not a day goes by—not a night—that I don't yearn to have her back with us, with me. Certain times will be harder to get through than others, and right now . . . well, yes, it is . . . tough."

He heard Taylor sniffling softly on the other end of the phone.

"Taylor, you need to stay focused on the here and now. Try to concentrate on your speech and school assignments and keep praying for

God's help. We're all going to get through this. You know that, right?" Doug said ever so tenderly.

"Yes," she said almost inaudibly.

"I love you, Taylor. I promise you, life is going to get better. I'd come take you to lunch or dinner today, but I need to see this hostage thing through, even though the case I'm working on may only be involved indirectly."

"That's okay, Dad. I don't have time for lunch anyway. You're right, Dad. It's hard, but we're going to be all right. I know we are. I better go now. I just needed to hear your voice and wanted you to know I love you."

"I love you too, honey. Do a good job on that speech. Call me later and tell me how it went. I want to hear all about it and how your audience reacted.

"Okay. Later."

They both made a kissing sound over the phone as though they were sending a kiss to each other through the phone wires. They had done that since Taylor was three years old. When he would be on a business trip, he would call the family every night to talk to each one of the kids. He always ended their conversation by telling them he loved them and then making a smacking sound over the phone. Taylor had continued to do that when talking to him over the phone every time they talked, even if they talked two or three times a day.

After Doug hung up, he decided to send a dozen pink roses to Taylor to lift her spirits. As the anniversary neared, he feared she might have an emotional setback if she had too much time to dwell on the recent past. She needed a distraction of some kind. As soon as this hostage ordeal ended, he would put his mind to work on a plan.

CHAPTER 54

Looking back at the church, Doug saw Jeff's Towing getting ready to remove the truck from the parking lot. The truck would be impounded to the sally port of the police station where the ID Bureau would search it thoroughly and check for fingerprints. The ID Bureau was the police department's crime scene unit and was responsible for maintaining police records. Since this was an emergency, no search warrant was required. Shortly, they may learn the name of one or both criminals and that could prove a big break for the authorities.

The note on the seat of the truck was of particular interest to Doug. If this guy's name was Rabone, then he was somehow connected to the Mabel Bender murder and may even be her murderer. It wouldn't bring Dan Bender's mother back, but it would give him closure.

And further, if indeed one of those men was Mabel Bender's murderer, the ladies inside that church could be in far greater jeopardy than originally believed, and authorities weren't dealing with simply young punks.

CHAPTER 55

At least twenty-five minutes had passed. Eddie and Bobby had quietly discussed the next plan for getting out of the church and out of the country. A successful escape would rest on the police fulfilling their promise. Knowing they would attempt to thwart the escape, Eddie and Bobby realized they would need to use some of the ladies as human shields as insurance for safe passage to the airport and for boarding the plane.

Olivia rose from her chair and walked up to the two men unassertively and with a coy demeanor.

"May I please use the restroom? We've all had to hold it for so long, we're all going to need the bathroom, you know."

"No. Go sit down. When we return to the sanctuary, we'll have a few of you go."

"A few? All of us have to go." Olivia advocated for the other women. She got a close up look at Bobby and noticed he was yawning and looking rather nonchalant.

Eddie and Bobby looked around the room, and all of the women were finished eating and were staring at the two men.

"Bobby, you pick ten women to go to the bathroom, and the other fifteen will go back to the sanctuary with me. I think it's time for us to put the fear of God in these women and the cops. They need to know we mean business. We've definitely got to get out of here before it gets dark, so I'm going to go back in the church and make a call to Web with our demands. They've strung us along enough. Now we give them a time line. If that doesn't work, Bobby, we're in big trouble. We'll have to take drastic measures. Make the women hurry. No washing hands—in and out. Got it?"

"Yepper!" said Bobby rather silly.

"And Bobby?"

"Yeah?"

"We may just have to kill one of the ladies to get their attention, so be ready."

CHAPTER 56

"I need ten ladies who have to go to the bathroom bad. Raise your hand," directed Bobby.

More than ten raised their hand, including Gracie. Gracie had already gone once, so he knew he shouldn't choose her. She needed assistance, and it would take too long, but he also was afraid that if something went wrong in the sanctuary and Eddie wanted to make a point by killing someone, he might pick Gracie. He didn't want Eddie to kill anyone. Wouldn't that compound their problems and motivate the police to force their way in to the church and take them by force? Earlier he and Eddie had agreed that no one would get hurt, and now, what was the easiest, most uncomplicated ruse might be turning into a deadly ruse and, of all things, backfiring on them.

Bobby stood up and felt light-headed. He had never felt that sensation before. He started to walk between the tables of ladies.

"Keep your hands up, girls. We're going to play Duck, Duck Moose, so when I tap you on the head, stand up and follow me to the toilette."

Bobby thought he was being humorous by calling it that, but actually the women were indignant by him calling them *moose*. Since he was the guy with the gun, they all planned to keep their mouths shut. They too were tired of these two young punks taking their purses, wasting their day, and putting them in danger. This needed to end soon, and they were counting on the police to do something about the situation. But if they didn't, perhaps they needed to find out if Donna Gifford had a plan and work with her.

Ten women were chosen, and Bobby waited until Eddie took the other ladies with him to the sanctuary. He could hear Eddie yelling at them to shut up. He heard Eddie threatening them, but he wasn't sure they were idle threats.

As Bobby stood in the hallway with the ladies standing in line waiting their turn to use the restroom, he could tell his vision was getting blurred. He had always been healthy and couldn't believe he was experiencing the light-headedness and blurred vision. Not only that, he was getting sleepy, very sleepy. He had close to eight hours of sleep last night even though he had been a little restless about their plans today. They always approached one victim at a time, never fifty or so.

Gracie Holstrom was coming out of the restroom, aided by Clare. Gracie looked at Bobby and aimed her walker at him.

"No. Stay over here, Gracie. Stay with me, honey."

Gracie ignored Clare and made her way to Bobby.

"Elvis, are you okay? You don't look so good. I loved lunch. Didn't yours set well with you? That cherry berry chiller was the best! Especially if you're like me and don't have teeth!"

By this point, Bobby ignored Gracie. It was almost like he had tuned her out. Finally, one by one, the ladies were lined up in the hallway ready to return to the sanctuary.

Bobby who stood behind the line directed the ladies to go into the sanctuary and return to their seats. Clare waited for Gracie to catch up to her, but Gracie lingered behind in order to be near Bobby. She noticed his balance was clearly off, so Gracie told him to grab on to her walker. She saw Gracie put her skinny little arm around Bobby's back to help support him while she held on to her walker with the other hand.

"Something's not right with you, Bobby. You need to see a doctor. Why don't you turn yourself in to the police. I'll come with you. Things will work out for the best that way. It's the right thing to do and you know it," she said persuasively.

Bobby never really responded, but he did lean on Gracie's walker.

Clare too realized something was wrong with the guy who called himself Elvis, but she pretty much knew his name was Bobby. The first thing that occurred to Clare was that maybe some of the food had been tainted by the police, but how could they know with any certainty that the bad guys would end up eating it? Or was it possible that Donna

Gifford slipped something in their food before delivery and arranged all of this? Clare didn't want Gracie involved as she wasn't sure how all of this was going to play out. One thing was for sure. This guy wasn't going to be on two feet much longer.

CHAPTER 57

As the women walked in to the sanctuary single file, they saw Eddie on the phone, and it was apparent he was vexed.

"Listen, Web, don't mess with me. We want out of here within the hour, or I swear these ladies are going to pay dearly."

"What do you mean, Eddie?"

"You know what I mean. We'll give you a reason to make our dreams come true, or you will live with a guilty conscience for the rest of your life when you realize not all women will come out alive."

"Getting you to the airport on a transport vehicle and on to a plane out of the country without a passport is complicated, John." Web made sure he kept using the pseudonym. "We're working as fast as we can so that no one gets hurt. But I can also assure you, if any of these ladies are harmed, all bets are off. Chances are you won't have a happy ending either, so let's work—"

"You listen to me, Web! You are in no position to threaten me. You have more to lose than I do. If these ladies get killed and the church is destroyed, everyone will blame you. Now shut up and get the job done! I don't want to hear from you until the plan is in place, and it had better be within an hour!"

"We'll do our best, John. Just stay calm and cool. We're doing our very best."

"You better hope your best is good enough, Webbie!" *Click.*

With the disconnect, everyone on the team looked at each other.

Dr. Brandon White thought for a moment. *These guys are getting tired, scared, and feeling trapped. They are getting to a breaking point.*

Since we know very little about them, we can't be sure how they will react as time goes by, and they aren't getting out of this church. But human nature is such that they will have to strut their power and superiority by doing something drastic to show they are in control. Does that mean they will kill one of the women? Possibly. And if not kill them, hurt them. They may let you hear her painful cries to elevate our fears and emotions and guilt. So I think we need to get the plan readied and get them out of the building and away from those women. However, the women are their collateral, so some of them may be used as human shields for their protection. We will have at least reduced the threat of the majority of the ladies and have saved the church unless they have booby-trapped the structure.

"Have we gotten a report yet on the truck? If our dogs didn't pick up a bomb scent in the truck, chances are there is no truth to their bomb threat. However, in case we miscalculate, the bomb squad is here and ready to enter the building to check for explosives once it's vacated, isn't it?"

"Yes, they're here and on standby," responded Web.

"Good. Well, let's hope we can stall them long enough to offer a feasible, credible plan to them."

"Commander Bates is working on it. I understand he got a close-up photo of both guys sent to him from Donna Gifford's spy pen. He's having their photos put on all of the TV stations—breaking news, of course—to see if anyone locally can identify them. That could be the big break we need. It's possible we already have a link with these guys to the recent Mabel Bender murder here in the city."

"Hmmm," responded Dr. White. "If this lead turns out to be true, we can add to their profile. Their capabilities of murdering some or all of these women just escalated. If they know we have that information, they will become skeptical of our allowing them to leave the country. We also know they wouldn't have any qualms about killing the women if they have murder already on their rap sheet. The risks and dangers have then increased."

"These guys sound more like uneducated punks. Do they have more criminal experience than we think, or are they talking tough to call our bluff?" inquired Web.

"As we know, the street-smart kids can work under the radar for a while, but eventually as they get bolder, They make a mistake, and they're welcomed into our judicial system. If we just had their names or knew if they were locals . . . Let's hope someone recognizes them on TV and steps forward."

CHAPTER 58

Chris Lambert had her bedroom television on while sorting the clean laundry that had just come out of the dryer. She was just starting to change the linens on their bed when Breaking News interrupted her program. She looked toward the screen and listened to the reporter as she described the scene at Gospel Bible Church. Both photos of the men came on the screen—very clear close-up photos—with an urgency for the public to look at them, and if anyone knew the identities of either or both of these men, they were to call the phone number at the bottom of the screen.

As soon as Chris saw the guy—the one who had the tan shirt with the red vertical stripes—she immediately connected him to the guy she saw talking to Mrs. Lawrence about her roof. The very next day, Mrs. Lawrence was dead. And now the same guy—at least he looked like the same guy albeit she had seen him from somewhat of a distance—was holding a bunch of elderly ladies hostage in a church. Surely this was the same guy. Mrs. Lawrence said his name was Joe. Chris also remembered he drove a black truck. She had given this report to the police at the time Mrs. Lawrence's murder was being investigated. In fact, it was on the very day her body had been discovered. Chris immediately wrote down the phone number at the bottom of the screen. She knew this may be something, or it may be nothing at all, but she just had to make the call.

The police asked her if she could come down to the station and discuss what she saw again in person. Meanwhile, the police pulled out the entire file on the Lois Lawrence murder. As they flipped through the paper file, they found Chris Lambert's report, which matched exactly what she had told them.

While there was no absolute proof of the connection, there were too many coincidences not to report this to Commander Bates.

Meanwhile, Chris called her dad who was a Summit County deputy and asked if he could accompany her to the police department to speak to the police. He assured her he would be in her driveway in ten minutes.

CHAPTER 59

Paul Conrad's cell phone rang as he was on his way to the Celeste Laboratory of Chemistry for his chemistry class at Ohio State University. He had been talking to one of his buddies who was on his way to the same building but for a different class.

As Paul pulled out his phone, he saw that the call was from Taylor. He stepped off the sidewalk to take the call and motioned for his friend to go on without him.

"Hi, Taylor. What's up?"

"Not much, bro. What's up with you?" she asked.

"I'm heading for chemistry class. We're taking a test in there, so I can't be late."

"Oh, all right. I was checking to see if you were okay."

"Sure, I'm fine. Why wouldn't I be?"

"Well, because . . . do you know what month this is?"

"Sure," he responded matter-of-factly. He wasn't following Taylor.

"Do you realize the date?" she asked with a frustrated tone.

"The date? Oh . . . oh, yeah. Who could forget that, Taylor? Are you okay, sis?"

"Yeah, I guess," she said. Paul could tell she was getting choked and about to cry.

"Listen, Taylor. It's a tough time. For all of us. None of us will ever forget what happened a year ago, but as time passes, it will get better. We're all going to get through this. I'm sure the first anniversary of Mom's death will be—"

"Murder," said Taylor.

"What?" asked Paul.

"Murder, not death. Mom was murdered." Taylor was being a stickler with the semantics.

"Yes, Mom's murder will be hard on us all as we think about it at this time. Try to keep busy and not dwell on it, to help you get through it. Have you talked to Dad recently?" Paul asked Taylor.

"I talk to Dad every day. He's busy right now. He's at a hostage site. I guess Gospel Bible Church is under siege with twenty-five ladies being held hostage. He didn't have time to talk."

"Really? Gospel Bible Church in Akron? That's wild. Isn't that the church Donna Gifford attends?"

"I don't know. Is it?"

"Yeah. I think she mentioned it once."

"Hmmm."

"Listen, Taylor, I love you and would really like to talk to you, but seriously, I can't be late for this test. I gotta run! If you need to, call Pastor Pascoe. I'm sure he or Holly can talk to you and help you through the next few days. If it's any consolation, Dad and I are feeling as morose as you about Mom. We're going to get through this, Taylor. It will get easier for us in time, okay?"

"Yeah, okay. Love you. Do well on your test, Paul."

"Thanks."

After Paul hung up, he began to hurriedly walk to his class, but he was troubled by Taylor's call. He could tell she was exceedingly sad. She had been through so much the night of their mother's murder, and months later, she was almost killed by Quinton Reed. She had received counseling by a professional psychologist and had help through Victim's Assistance, and of course, Pastor and Mrs. Pascoe were there for all of them, especially Taylor, every step of the way.

Paul felt bad having to cut off Taylor's call, for he was definitely sensitive to Taylor's needs and frailty at a time like this. There wasn't much he could do for Taylor when he was in Columbus and she was in Kent, Ohio, but he knew who could help her. He didn't know if his dad had his hands full with this hostage situation Taylor was telling him about or whether it was now over, but he decided to call his dad and, if need be, leave a voice mail. To his surprise, his dad picked up on the second ring.

"Hi, chick magnet."

"Hi, Dad. Are you okay?"

"Yes, I'm fine. Just a little busy."

"Me too. I've got a chemistry test in a few minutes. Taylor just called and told me about a hostage situation at Gospel Bible Church. Is it over now?"

"No, it's still ongoing, but I think SWAT is going to give it just a little more time and then they'll exercise their plan, whatever that is."

"Oh, so how are you involved in all of this?"

"Long story short, one of the perps may be the killer of one of the cases I'm working on. We're not sure, but it's possible. And then, well, Donna Gifford's mom was in the church for a Bible study when these two guys walked in. Donna Gifford managed to walk into the church in an effort to protect her mom and is now being held hostage as well."

"Oh, my. Does Taylor know that?" Paul asked.

"No."

"Good, because I think Taylor is bummed out about Mom right now. We're coming up to the anniversary of her death, and I think she's having a really tough time. You might need to stay close to the situation, Dad. She sounded like she's on the edge."

"Yes, I talked to her just a while ago, and I too sensed she was dwelling on the past too. She's in class right now, but I plan to surprise her this evening and take her to dinner. That is, if this hostage crisis is over. I can't in clear conscience leave Donna in there and simply walk away. Not with what she's done for our family."

Paul agreed with his father and understood the circumstances.

"I'm following you, Dad. Just keep in touch with Taylor. I think she's very fragile right now."

"Will do, son."

"I'm almost at my building now, Dad. Gotta take a chemistry test, so I've gotta run!"

"Do well, son."

"Thanks. I'll do my best!"

CHAPTER 60

After the black truck had been impounded to the sally port, it was secured and ready for inspection by the Police Identity Bureau. In Akron, their team was the crime scene unit, and they maintained all of the police records.

Since this case was one of imminent emergency, they followed Bates's explicit directions. The bomb-sniffing dog and his handler were the first ones to sniff the truck to see if it was booby-trapped in any way or if there might be or had been explosives inside the truck.

All indications from the canine were that the truck was void of explosives. They could now begin their internal search. On the seat beside the driver was a piece of paper that was mentioned by Bates. He wanted to know exactly what was on the note as soon as they found it. While one agent was removing items from the glove compartment, the other agent called Bates, having first read the note herself.

"Commander Bates. This is Diana Kelley. We have the note that was sitting on the truck seat. Shall I read it to you? I think it may be rather telling."

"Yes, read it to me, Diana."

"Here it is verbatim: 'Good morning, _____. This is Dexter Rabone from Eastern Capitol Bank. I'm the security director for the bank, and I'm wondering if I'm speaking to____?' There's a fill-in-the-blank for a name, most likely, Commander. Then the note continues: 'First, let me say there is no problem with your bank account whatsoever. Your money is perfectly safe. However, we have a problem with one of our bank tellers, and we have narrowed it down to one of two of them who work at the branch you deal with. We have been aware of the problem for several months, and now that we see what is happening, we need to set the bait so that we can terminate and prosecute this individual. This teller is focusing on our most valuable customers—the elderly. If I could very briefly and succinctly describe what is happening, we would certainly appreciate your help."

As the agent continued to read the rest of the script, aside from the person's response at the other end of what had to be a telephone conversation, Commander Bates was confident that these hostage takers were involved in the Mabel Bender murder.

He hung up and told the agents to call if they found the identities of these guys or anything else that might be pertinent.

Meanwhile, Bates called Doug Conrad on his cell and told him to come into the inner circle where he was. He needed a quick synopsis of the Mabel Bender murder case.

Doug was escorted into the inner circle and stood before Bates.

"Okay, Doug. Tell me the important facts of the Bender murder case."

"Mabel Bender withdrew $50,000 from her bank, Eastern Capitol Bank. The reason is unknown, but she told the teller it was to pay for her granddaughter's upcoming wedding, although she didn't have a granddaughter who was getting married. Bender was murdered in her home—shot—and, of course, there was no trace of the money. We believe Bender was either under duress or tricked into withdrawing the money. All family members were investigated thoroughly and exonerated as suspects.

"And the name that you gave me earlier?" Bates asked.

"The name was Rabone. Mabel Bender's son, Dan found that name on a Post-It in her handwriting in her kitchen by the telephone. He didn't recognize the name nor had he ever heard his mother speak of that name. We checked with Eastern Capitol Bank to see if it might be one of their employees since she had just taken out $50,000, but they had no one by that name working for them. Most likely Mabel was the victim of a scam."

"Well, Doug, we may have our scam murderers right here in the church. I think they were pulling another scam when the glory of the Lord came down and shone all around them," said Bates. "So our alleged purse snatching hoods are capable of so much more. This situation has now become a whole lot more complicated."

"Commander Bates? Lieutenant Boyer is on the phone. Says he needs to talk to you immediately. They got a call in from the newscast. They have a woman at the station who came in with her father, a deputy from Summit County. She says she may know something about one of the hostage takers. Boyer's on line 1 in the trailer."

Doug Conrad was left standing there while Bates quickly made his way into the SWAT vehicle. While Doug was in some ways hoping that this situation would solve the Bender murder and give Dan Bender closure to his mother's death, it was a situation that put Donna and her mom and the other ladies in clear and present danger.

CHAPTER 61

"This is Bates. What do you have for me, Lieutenant?"

"I have a lady by the name of Chris Lambert here in my office. Her eighty-year-old neighbor, Lois Lawrence, was murdered a couple of weeks ago, and when she saw the pictures of the two hostage takers, she recognized the one as being someone who was talking to Lawrence about putting on a new roof for her. Lawrence said his name was Joe. He never gave her a last name or a business card. He was seen driving a black truck with no business logo on it. What really caught her attention was the guy's shirt—it was tan with red vertical stripes. Which is what one of the perps is apparently wearing right now."

"Can she positively identify the guy?" asked Bates.

"She says she's about 95 percent certain. She's very sure of the shirt and the black truck. However, in our investigation of the Lawrence murder, no other neighbors had gotten new roofs put on as the guy had told Lawrence. Fifteen thousand dollars in cash was taken out of the bank the day before she was killed, and the money was never found. We're running with the idea she was caught in a scam."

CHAPTER 62

Everything that Bates heard about the Bender and now the Lawrence murder swayed him to believe that these two guys well may be their murderers. Their MO is targeting only old people. And if that is the case, their unsuccessful attempt to steal hand bags could lead them to kill these women if they felt they had nothing to lose.

Another thing that was still confusing Bates was that originally Donna Gifford had said that in her mom's text, she recognized one of the perps and his name was Eugene Fielder. Was this just another alias? Did this guy try to scam her in some way? And if so, under what circumstance? No criminal records had been found for a Eugene Fielder.

Bates quickly hashed all of this information over with Webster Thayer, Dr. White, and the other team members inside the vehicle. It was Dr. White's opinion that these men were going to panic soon if they weren't out of the building before evening. If they rushed the building, these guys wouldn't hesitate to kill some of the women or use them as human shields. His suggestion was to pretend to have transportation ready to deliver them to the Akron-Canton Airport and to convince them that a plane was prepared to shuttle them off to the Bahamas. When they step out of the church, the snipers need to disarm them via tear gas or bullet if they have to take the shot.

The nerves and patience of these women could start deteriorating quickly, and their responses to the pressure of their circumstances could lead to tragedy if police didn't act soon.

Bates was a patient and methodical man. He looked at a situation from everyone's point of view. There was little time to vacillate, but if these two punks didn't know they were suspects in at least two murders and only believed they were thought of as purse snatchers, they would have an easier time believing the police might let them go in lieu of losing lives. At this point, he had no proof whatsoever of any criminal activity these guys participated in prior to today. If SWAT took these guys out and they were only purse snatchers, that wouldn't bode well with the citizens of Akron nor the city.

Bates needed to get more pictures from Donna Gifford's spy pen. The police were processing their pictures in order to find matching mug shots and get their identification, but so far these guys were flying under the radar. If they moved around to different locations—city to city or even state to state—they could get by with their scams for years. Eventually punks like these guys make a mistake. Their greed level rises, and they are taken off the streets. Justice prevails.

CHAPTER 63

As soon as Bobby entered the sanctuary, he let go of Gracie's walker and dropped himself to the floor, leaning up against the altar.

Gracie was clearly confused as to what was happening to Bobby. Clare and Waneda quickly rushed to Gracie's side and guided her to the pew midway back where they had been sitting earlier.

"Something is going on with that boy. He told me he and his friend would be escaping by the 'skin of their feet.' Do you suppose someone—"

"Gracie, we need you to sit down and let the authorities do their job. I'm sure Elvis or Bobby or whoever he is will be just fine, okay dear?" said Clare.

Olivia turned back to Gracie and whispered, "Trust me, Gracie. The boy will be just fine. He probably got little sleep last night as he dreamt about stealing all of our hard-earned money. Lifting our heavy hand bags probably wore him out."

Donna Gifford saw that the guy named Bobby was almost asleep. His balance was off, and his emotions were flat. Had he shot up or something? If he had, his timing was surely bad. But this certainly could work for her good.

Weezie Bittner was a tall, heavy set African American lady who had a robust, commanding voice. When she sang solos at the church, her body swayed slowly, and her hands raised to the heavens. She knew how to put soul in her songs and make it come alive. When Weezie sang, you could feel the spirit of God move. She could bring the congregation to their feet and inspire them to join in the celebration of true worship.

Donna feared if she texted Bates, Eddie would hear her mother's phone make a sound. Weezie was sitting in front of her.

"Weezie. I need to text," Donna whispered to her. "Get a song going and hide my phone sound. Stay seated though."

"Okay, girl. You got it." Weezie made a humming sound as she searched for her starting note and then began:

We are standing on Holy Ground,
And I know that there are angels all around.
Let us praise Jesus now,
For we are standing in His presence,
On Holy Ground.

"Come on. Sing it with me, girls." The ladies began to join in.

We are standing in His presence,
We are standing in His presence,
Yes, we are standing in His presence on Holy Ground.

Before Donna could send a text to Bates, however, he sent her one. "Send pics of positions. Rushing 10 min. if CAK plan no work."

Donna replied, "Give more tim. 1 man ill-sleep?"

Bates: "Beliv both r killers. B carful.

When Donna looked up, she saw Eddie look over and see Bobby's head tipped to the side and heard him snoring. The look on Eddie's face was one of incredulity. He rushed over to Bobby and shook him but couldn't arouse him. Eddie would never leave Bobby behind, but he knew Bobby had to be alert and be a part of making their exit a successful one.

Eddie yelled to the women singing, "Shut up! Shut up now!"

The women froze with fear. They saw Eddie wield his gun from one side of the room to the other.

"Who's a nurse here? I need a nurse down here now!" he screamed. No one moved.

"There are no nurses among us," said Sue Myer.

"Then who's had first aid, something?" Eddie was panicking. He had never seen Bobby this way. What could be happening to him?

Still no one responded. Eddie walked over to Meg Foster sitting on the front row next to Kaitlyn. He grabbed her by her long, thick brown hair and pulled her out of her seat. He put a gun to the back of her head. Kaitlyn threw her hands over her mouth to stifle a scream.

"If someone doesn't come forward in two seconds to help my friend, I'm shooting her. Somebody here has to have some kind of medical background."

Kaitlyn kept her eyes on Meg, fearful that she would truly be shot before their very eyes. She saw a dark spot around the crotch of Meg's beige slacks appear and realized Meg had just wet her pants. It broke her heart, and she knew she couldn't take the pressure any longer.

Kaitlyn Kidwell stood up. "I had a first-aid class and CPR when I was in high school, but I'm thirty years old now. It's been a long time. I can look at him, but I doubt I will know what's wrong with him," she said.

"Come look." He pushed Meg back and told her to return to her seat. Tears were silently flowing down her cheeks. You could see she was so scared that not even a sound came out of her.

This poor girl was so traumatized, Sue Myer feared that if Meg survived today, she would probably never work another day at the church.

"I think he's just sleeping," said Kaitlyn.

"Wake him up," demanded Eddie.

"Wake him up?" she asked.

"You heard me. If he's sleeping, he should be able to wake up, right?" Eddie responded sardonically.

"Yes, I guess," said Kaitlyn.

Kaitlyn smacked him lightly on the cheek. No response. She smacked him a little harder on the other cheek. Still no response. She punched him a little harder in the ribs. She tried lifting his eyelids, but his eyes just seemed to be in a daze. He made a slight moan that was barely audible, but Eddie heard it.

Kaitlyn knelt beside Bobby and felt his pulse. It was quite slow. His heartbeat was slow as was his respirations. He actually looked like he was sleeping, but that just didn't make sense. How could he sleep at a time like this?

"He's just not responding. I'm sorry. I don't know what's wrong with him. I think he's sleeping."

Every eye in the sanctuary was on Eddie and Bobby. The room was eerily silent. Eddie became livid. He kicked Bobby in his leg but not terribly hard. Just enough to arouse him. "Hey, wake up, man!" Still nothing. Eddie realized that Bobby must have been sedated. They sneaked something in his food. But if they did, why wasn't it in his food too? It had to be from the McDonald's food. Eddie looked back through the ladies.

"So where's the McDonald's girl?"

Donna had already taken her gun out of her ankle holster and put it in her waistband. She handed her Mom's cell phone back to her, having just sent Bates a quick text.

Donna raised her hand.

"You put something in the food, didn't you?" Eddie asked Donna.

"No, I didn't. I swear I didn't."

"Then the police put something in it," Eddie accused.

"No, they couldn't have. The food never left my possession once I left McDonald's. As I said, I work the register. I had nothing to do with food preparation. No one at my restaurant would have tainted the food. I know that for a fact. The franchise would close up if we were ever caught doing such a thing. Besides, the way they packaged the food, they'd have no idea which sandwiches would go to which people."

Donna was trying to process what was happening to Bobby herself. She silently agreed he was probably drugged, but it wasn't by the police or the McDonald's employees. That would mean it had to come from one of the ladies inside the church. How crafty. As Donna thought about who it might have been, Olivia Rainey came to mind. Her eyes moved around the audience until she found Olivia Rainey sitting next to the pastor's wife. Olivia's eyes met hers, and she saw Olivia wink. Then she knew what most likely had happened.

Olivia felt badly that she hadn't been able to reach Donna in the dining room or the restroom to tell her what she'd done. She could tell Donna understood the meaning of her wink. She also was troubled that Donna was getting falsely accused of drugging Elvis, but she knew she would confess if Donna was going to be in serious danger.

Eddie was getting more enraged by the second as he watched his friend lying on the floor. Their plan was falling apart, and this newest problem might change everything here at the end. The game plan was breaking down. He had never anticipated this problem. If the police were dealing with only one person now instead of two, it would be so much easier to overwhelm him and take him down. All negotiations would be off. There was no way he was leaving Bobby behind, but he knew he couldn't carry him out and keep a gun pointed at the women who would serve as shields for them. In fact, some of these women were frisky—and the big black lady looked like she could whoop Muhammad Ali during his peak. If those women turned on him at the same time, they could probably bring him down.

He and Bobby had planned to use the younger women, the young mothers who had more to lose, as their shields. Because they needed to stay alive for their families, they would cooperate fully. The value of their life was worth more to the authorities, so they wouldn't be inclined to risk their safety in order to assassinate him and Bobby.

Eddie turned to Meg Foster and pulled her to her feet. "I know you have to have coffee somewhere in this office. Bring a pot and a cup back in here. Oh, and also bring a pitcher of ice water."

"I can't carry that all by myself," Meg said. Frustrated, Eddie looked at Kaitlyn.

"You go with her and help. If you try to escape, I'm putting a bullet between sweet Gracie's eyes. Do you understand? And that will be just for starters."

Both girls nodded their head.

"Now hurry!" Eddie yelled. "Move it!"

CHAPTER 64

Bates received a quick report on Bobby's condition from Donna's text. As happenings inside the church started to unravel for the perps, John's behavior would become more erratic and unpredictable. Bates wanted to get a text message to Gifford to warn her that within minutes, they would be storming the building and to sit tight. They were depending on their thermal imaging, but her spy pen was allowing them to see everyone's location.

Bates was informing all of the snipers positioned on the rooftops of nearby buildings and those who were stationed inside buildings on the upper floors to get ready for his order.

The reporters and cameramen were ordered to move away and beyond the outer circle for their protection and for other reasons. Only SWAT cameras would be videotaping the live action. If for some reason things went sour, lawsuits were a sure thing. They needed no help from the liberal press.

Bates whispered a prayer that no one would get hurt—not one female hostage, none of his men, and neither of the hostage takers. That would be the ideal outcome. He was the commander, and the buck would certainly stop with him. He had an unblemished record up to now, and he wanted to keep it that way, so he needed to stay focused.

He had a brief but private talk with Webster Thayer as to Web's next and final conversation with John Wayne. There was a meeting of the minds between the two men. The final step of this escapade was about to begin. Twenty-seven lives were at risk. Let the stress begin.

CHAPTER 65

Sitting directly in front of Donna Gifford, right on the aisle, was Fannie Furman, and next to her was Weezie Bittner. Fannie was in her late seventies and walked with a three-legged Flex Stick walking cane. She had it right next to her in the aisle so it would be convenient to her and not bother the other ladies in the pew.

Eddie watched Meg and Kaitlyn head for the lunch room for coffee and ice water. Both girls whispered softly to each other on their way to the lunch room.

"We could make a 911 call quickly and let police know there is one man down. You think we could?" asked Meg.

"If we do anything other than what he said, he might really kill Gracie," reasoned Kaitlyn. "I think something is going to happen in the next thirty minutes, Meg. The police are getting ready to do something. I sense it, don't you?"

Tears were streaming down Meg's cheeks as she was grabbing the coffeepot from the coffeemaker. It had been on for hours and surely had to be yucky!

"I keep wondering how my little Allison is doing. She's only five months old. There's so much I should have taught Brad about warming her food or her bottle. I just never thought there was a chance something would happen to—"

Kaitlyn interrupted her. "Meg, we're all going to get out of here alive. Hold on to your faith. God's never going to leave us or forsake us." She then put her arms around Meg and gave her a warm, reassuring hug.

"Hang in there, sweetie! Now, let's go so Gracie can live to celebrate her one hundredth!"

Meg smiled at that as she brushed away her tears. "Okay. I'm putting on my coat of courage."

"Good girl!"

"And Kaitlyn?"

"Yes?"

"You probably saved my life by stepping forward back there. You put your life on the line for me. Thanks!" Meg said with tears in her eyes.

"As we know, Meg, 'There is no greater love than this . . .' but we both came out okay, so God is here and watching over us! 'Be not afraid.'"

Chapter 66

Meanwhile Eddie had turned his attention back to face Donna after the two girls had headed for the kitchen.

"I don't believe you. Something was in the food or drink, and you either did it or you know who did." He started to step into the aisle but realized if he went to Donna, the ladies could surround him and possibly overpower him. Come up here," Eddie demanded.

He had his gun cocked and pointed straight at her. She didn't know how good of a shot Eddie was, but she did know how accurate she was. It may be a choice between kill or be killed in the next few seconds. "Remember, Donna, no one wants bloodshed in the church," she recalled Sue Myer whispering earlier to her. You don't always have a choice, however. She had hoped to get close enough to him in order to knock or kick the gun out of his hand and put a few of her judo moves on him to disarm him. The opportunity hadn't availed itself, however, but she was soon going to have a reason to step closer. She could tell at this point he was losing his cool. She needed to be prepared because anything could happen.

She started to step in to the aisle. Eddie looked back at Bobby. Bobby actually looked like he was in a deep, deep coma. How could everything go so wrong when they were so close to getting out of here? It was this chick who was going to bring them down. A stupid, imbecile, McDonald's idiot! If he was arrested, police might connect him and Bobby to the two old ladies murdered, and they would either die in prison or be executed. No way he could let that happen. This bitch had ruined everything, and he was going to make her pay!

He took three aggressive steps forward with his gun cocked and pointed in Donna's direction. Donna knew it was time to act. She pulled her gun out of her waistband, and as she stepped out into the aisle, her right foot got tangled in Fannie's three-legged walking cane, and she lost her balance. She felt a powerful shove in her back. Her right arm that held her gun dropped downward, and she fell to the floor. She heard her mother scream, "Noooooo!"

Eddie aimed his gun and pulled the trigger as Stella hurriedly stepped into the aisle. Eddie fired the gun, hitting Stella instead of Donna. Stella dropped to the ground. Not a sound was uttered from her, not even a groan. The ladies saw blood spurting from Stella and knew an artery had been hit. She would need help immediately, or else she would bleed to death. These men had come into their church and violated it and them. Enough already! Terror gripped the women, but so did anger.

Not the least concerned that he had just shot someone, Eddie turned and walked rapidly to the front of the room where he had been perched much of the time. Meg and Kaitlyn were coming into the sanctuary and witnessed the shooting. Both girls froze.

Eddie pointed the gun at them.

"Pour a cup of coffee and try to get it in him. Meanwhile, throw some ice water on him."

Meg Foster lifted the lid on the coffeepot, and in one swift movement hurled the steaming coffee in Eddie's face. Kaitlyn then swung the pitcher of ice water in his face. The sound of the impact convinced her Eddie would be losing a few teeth. He was completely taken by surprise and dazed by the impact to his face.

Ruthann Hanna stood up in the second row and hurled a hymnal at Eddie, hitting him in the back, followed by Addie Bartow who threw one and hit him in the arm. This might be their one and only chance of disarming this guy. The ladies got out of their seats and were heading straight for Eddie who was bent over in pain. His face was red and blistered from the coffee, and his eyelids were swelling shut. He had dropped his gun on the floor. Sue Myer picked it up and stepped away.

Jon Bates was seeing and hearing some of this from Donna's spy pen. Then he heard Donna shout in a very controlled voice, "Time to get in here. One victim shot, one perp unconscious, and the other perp temporarily disabled. Need paramedics quickly!"

As soon as Bates heard the gunshot and the women screaming, he had already ordered his men to enter the church. He also called for the paramedics to move in closer as well. Jon knew every hostage situation was unique, but he had never seen anything like this. His motto had always been "Expect the unexpected." Today was that day.

This moment could have turned in to a melee, but then the women heard the biggest crashing sound, and in came the SWAT team with MP5s in hand storming the place like ants on a sandwich on a hot summer's day. The relief on the women's faces was priceless.

Meg Foster was just standing there squeezing the empty coffee pitcher and crying. The agent had to pry the pitcher from her hand and assist her to the front pew. He reached down and whispered something to her. She shook her head affirmatively, and he patted her on the shoulder. Kaitlyn then went and sat down beside Meg and embraced her.

"You saved us, Meg. Your brave action saved us! You immobilized the guy and gave the police the break they needed!"

"Yes, but Stella's been shot. Is she dead?"

"I don't know, but he shot her before he could get close enough to us so that you could throw the coffee in his face. More of us could have gotten hurt if it wasn't for you. All I know is that you were our angel today that God used to help get us out of this situation."

"Yeah? Can you believe it?"

Kaitlyn laughed for the first time in hours. "Well, God works in mysterious ways, doesn't He?"

"He sure does. I might stop shaking tomorrow," said Meg.

"You'll stop shaking when you hold Allison and Brad."

"You're right about that."

CHAPTER 67

Medics rushed in and went straight to Donna Gifford who was applying pressure to her mom's arm. An artery apparently was severed. Immediately Donna stepped aside, and they took over. Out came some hemostatic gauze to stop the bleeding and the CAT, which is 100 percent effective in occluding blood flow in upper extremities. Donna watched as they put an internal band around her mother's bicep to provide circumferential pressure to her extremity. She knew her mom would be getting the emergency care she needed to keep her alive.

The authorities told the women to quickly be seated. Three paramedic vehicles were on site. Two paramedics began working over Stella LaMarre to stabilize her while two others hovered over Bobby. Olivia Rainey yelled out, "He's really okay. He took two three-milligram tablets of Restoril." The paramedics shook their heads and actually started laughing.

Two paramedics were treating Eddie for his burns. The officers were standing around Eddie who was now handcuffed and seated on the altar looking like a burnt offering. They had done a thorough body search of him first before allowing the paramedics to treat his burns and bleeding, busted mouth. He would need to be taken to the hospital for his injuries. The unconscious guy was also handcuffed and would need his condition assessed at the hospital.

The women were so relieved their captivity was now over. They had endured five harrowing hours with these thugs. The women turned to watch the paramedics working over Stella. They saw the tormented look on Donna's face as she was terrified for her mother's life.

Weezie Bittner knew everyone needed to calm down and give thanks. Someone heard her hum as she once again found her starting note and then led in a song that would inspire the ladies to join her.

Surely the presence of the Lord is in this place,
I can feel His mighty power and His grace.
I can hear the brush of angel's wings,
I see glory on each face.
Surely the goodness of the Lord is in this place.

The women were singing in harmony, and the SWAT team just stood there in silence and respect as these ladies found their own serenity. The harmony was so perfect Bates thought he was listening to the Von Trapp family. As the men scanned the twenty-five ladies sitting in the pews, it wasn't hard to spot Gracie Holstrom. She was sitting between two ladies who had their arm around her. A lady sitting behind her also had her hand on Gracie's shoulder. As the women sang, tears of joy and thanksgiving were streaming down their faces. Gracie wasn't crying however. She was enjoying all of the love and attention she was getting. Her countenance was one of peace and contentment.

Several SWAT members had searched every part of the church. The bomb squad had also worked its way to each part of the building so that it was declared safe.

The only serious injury that occurred among the women was to Stella LaMarre, and Bates now understood what led to Eddie's sudden panic. They were almost ready to talk Bobby and Eddie out of this building safely when things went awry. Bates knew he would later second-guess his strategy if Donna Gifford's mother died. But if these two guys did kill Mrs. Bender and Mrs. Lawrence, putting continued heat on them sooner could have escalated the situation into something much worse.

His report would be long. He would have to get testimony from each of the twenty-five ladies. Fortunately for the spy pen, they had all of the evidence—visual and audio recordings—to convict these guys. Then if these guys confess or are proven to be the murderers of the other two ladies, today will have been a bonanza for SWAT and the Akron Police Department. It certainly wasn't a typical day for his SWAT team, but their goal has always been to keep the citizens of Akron safe. He knew that at the end of the day as he drove home to be with his wife and three kids, Akron was now a safer place than it had been this morning.

CHAPTER 68

Doug Conrad had remained in the inner circle but outside the SWAT vehicle. He knew something had happened to accelerate the rush into the building, and it couldn't be good. He was feeling the tension building up inside of him.

Within seconds, a door had been broken, and the team armed with MP5s had entered. He heard no gunfire, but he saw the paramedics rush in. Obviously there was an emergency inside that led SWAT to get in there.

It was only minutes before he saw someone brought out on a transport and saw paramedics frantically working over a body. Following the transport was Donna who was about to get in to the ambulance with the paramedics.

"Donna!" Doug called out.

"Follow us, Doug! We're going to Akron General."

"Okay."

The siren and lights came on, and the ambulance sped away.

CHAPTER 69

Both Gospel Bible Church and Akron General Medical Center were in downtown Akron, so it didn't take Doug long to arrive at the hospital. He parked in the ER parking lot. When he got into the ER, there was no sign of Donna. The room was full of people either waiting to be seen or family or friends waiting for someone in the ward who was already being cared for.

"I'm Doug Conrad. An ambulance just arrived with a lady whom I'm assuming may be Stella LaMarre. She would have been accompanied by Donna Gifford."

"Are you family, sir?"

"No. Donna is a coworker and friend."

Doug realized what the lady was getting at. If you're not family, then everything is confidential and he would be told to have a seat and join the army of waiters.

"I'm sure Mrs. Gifford will be returning soon to the waiting room. Have a seat, Mr. Conrad, and I'm sure it won't be too long of a wait." The lady behind the desk then realized who Doug Conrad was.

"Thank you," Doug said, although he was feeling frustrated not knowing anything.

"And Mr. Conrad?" said the lady behind the desk.

"Yes?"

"It's very nice to meet you. I prayed very hard for you and your family when your wife was missing. I was hoping for a happier outcome, but I admired your courage and strength through it all. I hope I haven't made you sad. I'll let Mrs. Gifford know you're out here."

"No need. I'm sure she will realize I'm out here and will come out when she can."

"Yes, sir. There is free coffee and hot tea around the corner in the kitchenette area. Help yourself."

"Thanks."

CHAPTER 70

Stella was rolled to bed 3 in the ER and would be taken to the operating room in a few minutes. The trauma team was waiting for the ambulance to arrive to begin their work. One was typing her blood while another was changing her IV bag and another nurse was taking over applying pressure on her bicep where the artery had been severed. Still another was getting her prepped for the operating room. She had been stabilized actually in the ambulance en route to AGMC and had actually gained consciousness.

Donna was given only a minute to speak to her mom before they wheeled her onto the elevator that would open into the operating room. Had Stella not gotten the quick emergency care she did, she would unquestionably have bled out and died.

"Oh, Mom, why did you step in the way? Why?" Donna was squeezing her mother's hand so affectionately.

Her mother smiled and had a look of peace on her face. "I couldn't let him shoot you, Donna. I'd never forgive myself. Besides, 'there is no greater love than this, that a man lay down his life for a friend . . .' or daughter. I'll be fine, sweetheart. Did the other ladies get out of the church unharmed?"

"Yes, Mom, they did."

"And Gracie is okay?"

"She's fine. She'll have quite a story to tell her friends in the nursing home. You are going to be fine too, Mom. I'll be praying for you. Stay strong. I still need you so." Donna was lovingly stroking her mother's forehead and pushing her hair away from her face.

"It's time to take her to the OR, ma'am. You can wait in the waiting room. Give your name to the attendant at the front desk, and the doctor will talk to you as soon as he comes out."

"Okay. Fix her up and bring her back to me."

Donna leaned over the gurney and gave her mother a kiss on the cheek and a thumbs-up.

"I love you, Mom."

"I love you too, honey."

Donna looked back as her mom and the team were turning the corner heading for an open elevator that was awaiting them.

"Stella, we're going to fix you up. Before you know it, you will be like brand-new," Donna overheard the nurse say in a calm and confident manner. She leaned against the wall and just sobbed. Her heart ached for her mother who had taken a bullet for her. Life takes so many unexpected surprises. The morning starts out fine. You go to work, or in her mom's case, to church, and in what should have been the safest place ever—church—she gets her hand bag stolen and gets shot. There had to be a lesson or moral in here somewhere, but she was too shaken to process it right then. She would need to think about that one for a long time. The fact that her mom hadn't bled out and was still alive was more than enough to be thankful for. She saw the rainbow in today's events and felt God's presence with her and her mom.

"I did feel the brush of angels' wings this afternoon, Lord. I have just one more request. Please, dear God, pull Mom through this." With tears streaming down her face, she stepped out of the ER and into the waiting room.

CHAPTER 71

As soon as Doug saw Donna, he walked over to her immediately. Ever since she returned to Akron, it seemed like she was in one crisis after another. It seemed to follow her and Doug. Despite all that, if anyone was more grounded or anchored than Doug, she didn't know who it would be.

Donna had been strong for her mother and the other ladies at Gospel Bible. She really believed that the way things had been playing out, everything was going to come out peaceably. The negotiators were apparently keeping the hostage takers calm and feeling like they had a way out. She wasn't part of the team, but from her past experience, she knew that by her getting in there she could get up close and personal and assess the situation for the team. If anything did go awry, she figured she could disarm them if given the right opportunity. However, Olivia's interference tipped the balance, causing the situation to become chaotic and erratic. She couldn't have possibly calculated that. A piece of the puzzle had been missing, but she knew when Bobby lost consciousness, a dilemma had been created. One thing she could say unequivocally, Akron had one terrific SWAT team and police force. What went wrong today was not their fault, but she knew they would reevaluate their steps since there was a casualty. All incidents like this are teachable moments for everyone involved.

She and Doug sat on a love couch. She tried to say something to Doug, but tears began to stream down her face once again. She was unable to speak as a result of being so overwhelmed. She kept shaking her head back and forth as though saying, "How could this have happened. How could it?" Doug put his hand on her shoulder in a loving way, but then all her pent up emotions of the day exploded. At first he felt helpless and awkward, but she seemed so defenseless and vulnerable. Without becoming too analytical, he put his strong arms around her and held her close, letting her cut loose. And cut loose she did. She remained speechless for minutes before she could even make an audible sound. He gave her all the time she needed.

"What happened in the church, Donna?" Doug asked when she calmed down. "Is it Stella? Did she get hurt?" he asked quietly.

"It happened so fast, Doug. Things were going along all right, but then disaster struck. Everything changed in the blink of an eye. One minute things were in control, and then the next minute they weren't."

"Hmmm," said Doug. "My dad used to say that if things change in the blink of an eye, don't worry. God never blinks."

Donna smiled as she thought about that concept. The problem is when things are changing so quickly, you have little time to think about that."

"So what happened in there?" Doug asked again.

"I was getting accused of tainting the food, which of course I didn't do."

"So who did?" Doug asked with a great deal of curiosity.

"Olivia Rainey threw in a few of her Restoril pills as condiments on Bobby's sandwich, but I didn't know she did that. So then he falls into a deep, deep sleep. John blames me, and in a panicked state comes toward me with his gun cocked ready to shoot me. I know I'm going to have to shoot him, but I stumbled over Fannie Furman's three-legged cane, and my mom sees what is happening and shoves me so that John's bullet intended for me actually hits her."

"How bad is it?"

"He got her in an artery. On her bicep. I saw blood coming from her chest. I think the bullet may have hit her in the chest too. She dropped immediately and went into shock. Thank God for the quick rescue. She has a good chance for recovery, I think, unless something else is going on that I don't know about. My mom thought she was saving my life—and probably did—but she jeopardized her own. I don't know if I can ever get over that, Doug."

"Well, I'm told that time heals everything, so we need to give time, time."

"Are you there yet?" asked Donna.

"No, I'm not there yet," he said. Donna could hear regret and sadness in his voice. "As you know, life isn't tied with a bow, Donna, but it's still a gift, so we just need to keep counting our blessings as they come, and they do come."

Donna gave that more thought. If anyone had been through a terrible crisis, it was Doug. Who knew better how to weather the storm? She shook her head in agreement as she let showers of blessings flow down her face.

"Today no one died, and whatever doesn't kill you makes you stronger," said Doug. He took hold of her hand and held on. In a strange way, it felt right, and she was glad Doug was there.

CHAPTER 72

T wo hours later, Donna was called to the front desk of the waiting room and informed that her mother was now out of surgery and that as soon as Dr. DuVall cleaned up, he would meet her in Conference Room One to go over her mother's condition.

She turned to Doug.

"Will you come in with me?" she asked.

"Sure. If you'd like me to," Doug said.

Donna nodded her head, and together they walked into conference room 1. She sat down in one of the comfortable chairs, positioning herself toward a dry board that was on the wall in case the doctor diagrammed what he had found and done in surgery. Doug sat in the matching chair to her right. They sat in silence. Doug studied Donna. He could see that her mind was racing inside her, probably anticipating what the doctor would say and wondering how bad it would be. She had tried to keep her emotions in check, but now as they were drawing closer to the finish line, he sensed her anxiety and saw the fear beginning to wash over her.

Doug reached over and took her hand.

"I feel confident that everything is going to come out all right, Donna. From the time she was shot, the right attention and care was given to her. That didn't happen by accident. You know that. Besides that, she has a lot of people praying for her."

Donna knew what Doug was saying, and she drew strength from his insight. She took a deep breath, and then she heard a quick knock on the door.

CHAPTER 73

T he door opened, and in walked the doctor in his surgical scrubs. Dr. DuVall was a vascular surgeon who had a reputation for being one of the best in the Akron area. He introduced himself and then took a seat across from Donna and Doug.

"Things came out surprisingly well. Your mom is going to have a full recovery. I don't anticipate any complications or problems that would hinder her from full use of her arm. The bullet tore through her brachial artery in her bicep. I had to clean that out. We did have to give her a couple of units of blood due to the loss, of course, but in twenty-four to forty-eight hours that should make her feel a lot better.

"There was no nerve damage, and most of the muscle was intact. What damage was done will heal on its own. We'll keep her in the hospital for a couple of days until we're satisfied she's got good circulation to her lower arm and hand. Her arm will be in a sling for a while as we try to keep her arm immobile and give it time to heal.

"The bullet continued through her bicep and grazed her chest, doing superficial damage to her right breast. The bleeding there would make it look worse than it actually was. We cleaned and dressed that. That will heal in several weeks, but she'll need to change the dressing once a day and use antibiotic ointment on it once or twice a day.

"It will take several days to a week for her strength to return. The blood loss caused her to go into shock, and that's clearly a trauma to the body. She'll just need some time. I understand she's been through quite an ordeal today."

"She sure has, along with twenty-four other ladies."

"Well, she was conscious when we rolled her into the operating room and actually seemed quite calm and at peace. She told us she had a higher power watching over her today and that she was not afraid. So I'm sure her strong faith in God and good attitude will speed her recovery along.

"In a couple of hours you'll be called back to the recovery room and can see her. Do you have any questions?"

"No. I think you covered things quite well, Dr. DuVall. Thank you so much for taking such good care of her. Thank you for what you do."

"You bet!" He stood up and shook her hand and then patted Doug on the shoulder as if to say, "It's nice that you could be here for her today." It was obvious Dr. DuVall recognized Doug Conrad.

CHAPTER 74

Donna and Doug stepped out and into the Waiting Room and were met by a deluge of Donna's friends. Reverend Myer and Sue were there as were Waneda Robinson, Clare Rouse, Kaitlyn Kidwell, Amanda Armstrong, Olivia Rainey, Weezie Bittner, and Jon Bates who was with Officer Mike Walsh. All were anxious to get a full report on Stella. Donna was overwhelmed that so many of the women from Gospel Bible were there after the grueling and frightening day they all had had. She understood why Commander Bates and Officer Walsh were there. Bates didn't look too pleased with her and she knew why. Yes, they were concerned about Stella, but they had questions for her and her mom and needed to fill out a tentative report. That would have to be done in the next day or two however.

Bates had managed to confiscate her spy pen before she climbed into the ambulance with her mother. He needed Donna to connect some dots, but he was mostly interested in how Donna's mother recognized one of the assailants and believed his name to be Eugene Fielder.

Donna admitted she hadn't had an opportunity to question her mom about that either, but questions for her mom would have to wait until tomorrow after her anesthesia wore off. Bates was curious as to why these guys had targeted the church.

Bates knew Donna had a spy pen on her. He had figured out the frequency it was on before Donna had entered the church against his directive. Because her mother was one of the hostages, it made it unacceptable to allow her to assist in the situation. She might be too emotional and react in a way she ordinarily wouldn't if no family member was involved. Sometimes drastic measures are needed for drastic times, but if things had gone terribly wrong and if Donna had been shot herself, Bates would have a lot of explaining to do for having used someone outside their team to get near a danger zone. He clearly had not endorsed her going in.

Bates had actually told Donna not to enter the building. She was just to take the food up to the door to try to get a glimpse of the men and get a quick photo if possible. But in reality, Bates had an idea that Donna would go in since her mother was in there and if an opportunity afforded itself. After talking with the ladies and thanking them for coming, Donna insisted they all go home and try to relax and get some rest. Pastor Myer said a prayer on behalf of them and Stella, and then one by one, they hugged Donna and reluctantly left, promising to return tomorrow.

An hour later, Donna and Doug were permitted to see Stella in the recovery room. As soon as they walked in, they saw Stella in a hospital bed isolated from two other patients in the ward. She was hooked to an IV but wasn't on any oxygen. In fact, she was pretty alert for just having surgery.

Donna leaned over the railing of her mom's bed and kissed her on the cheek.

"Dr. DuVall said you're going to have a full recovery, Mom. The worst is behind you."

"So no one else got hurt?" Stella asked.

"No. No one else, Mom."

"Good."

"Mom, may I ask you a question?"

"Sure."

"Did you know one of those guys? In your text to me, you said his name was Eugene Fielder."

"No. I didn't, but Waneda Robinson recognized him. Apparently, one day last week, he drove by Waneda's house when she was working in the yard. He offered to help her do yard work or any heavy work in the house that she might need as he was out of work and could use some extra money. He told her his name was Eugene Fielder."

"So you had never laid eyes on him before today?"

"No. I think Waneda sensed something wasn't authentic about him, so she didn't hire him. You'll have to ask her. I texted his name quickly in case it helped.

"Sweetie, you need to go home and get some rest. Besides, Blaze and Chunx need to be taken out. Oh dear, poor Chunx—he can't hold it forever."

"I'll take care of Chunx, Mom. Don't worry. We're going to leave you so you can get some rest, but I will be back in the morning.

"Sleep well, Mom. You'll be home soon. The doctor promised."

Her mom gave her a weak wave with her left hand and blew her a kiss good-night.

She could now leave the hospital knowing her mother was being well cared for. It truly had been an exhausting day.

CHAPTER 75

Doug drove Donna to her home, leaving her car at the church. Donna had a 9:00 a.m. appointment at the police station with Bates, and Doug promised to pick her up early and take her to the church to retrieve her car. Emotionally she was drained and, understandably, didn't want to go back to the site where her mom had been shot.

It was 9:30 p.m., and both of them were hungry and emotionally exhausted.

"After you take the dogs out, would you like to go to the Waterloo Restaurant, and we can grab something to eat?" Doug asked.

"I'm starving, but I think I'd rather stay home. I can pop a few chicken pot pies in the microwave for us, if that works for you?"

"Perhaps you'd rather just have some time alone, Donna. I'm sure there's something in my frig I can find when I get home," said Doug.

"Well, actually, I don't want to be alone. I'd like you to stay for a while, if you can," Donna responded honestly.

"Pot pies sound great to me," Doug said with a convincing smile.

As Donna was unlocking the side door to her house, she could hear Chunx barking and stirring around on the other side of the door.

"I'll hurry and let Chunx out, Doug. Would you mind reaching up on a shelf above the refrigerator and grab a treat out of his cookie jar?"

"No problem."

"You'd better step aside," Donna warned. Doug obeyed. He remembered his first experience with the mastiff and didn't wish to repeat it.

As soon as the door opened, Chunx came charging out and headed for a specific place in the yard to do his number. Blaze followed. While they were going, Donna decided to walk to the mailbox and bring in the mail.

Doug actually had to get on his tiptoes to reach the jar that contained the giant milk bones. His body was pressed against the refrigerator with his right arm stretched as far as it could be extended to grab hold of the milk bone. Before he could even get his heels to the floor and bring his arm down, he felt his entire body being pressed into the refrigerator by something huge with nasty breath. He saw a paw on each side of his head and felt its breath on the back of his neck. This mammoth head lunged for the bone in Doug's right hand, and he was more than willing to surrender it. Doug was pinned to the refrigerator and at the mercy of the dog until it was ready to free him. The dog really wasn't aggressive, just overly eager to get what he valued as his. Nevertheless, Doug was unable to move and, again, was frozen with fear.

Donna walked into the house while glancing through her mail. When she looked up, she saw Doug pinned to the refrigerator by Chunx whose body was almost covering Doug's.

"Chunx! Get down!" The dog obeyed immediately.

"Oh, Doug, I'm so sorry! Are you okay? I didn't realize he would come back to the house so soon. I thought I had time to get my mail in."

Doug tried not to look afraid although he was sure his blood pressure would be off the chart.

"Do you mind if I use your bathroom, Donna?"

"Of course not, Doug. It's down the hall and to the left."

As he left, Donna smiled. Until people came to know Chunx, he took some getting used to. His size alone was what was so intimidating. He was really a gentle giant and a great protector. She was hoping, in time, Doug and Chunx could become friends.

When Doug returned to the kitchen, the color had come back to his cheeks.

"I'm thinking Chunx could use a good mouthwash, Donna."

Donna laughed. "Coincidentally, he's scheduled at Metropolitan Veterinary Hospital to have his teeth cleaned next Tuesday. Dr. Gary Riggs, our vet, will clean his teeth and remove several cysts, but other than that, Chunx is one healthy guy!"

"Yes, he certainly is," said Doug with conviction.

As Doug waited for the pot pies to come out of the oven, he looked around the house. It was a very nice, well-kept ranch home. The rooms were spacious and the walls faux painted with a rich beige. The furniture was upholstered in warm colors and relaxing patterns. A large sectional couch hugged part of two walls. A large bookcase took up much of one wall. It contained many books but held a lot of family photos as well. The art on the walls was tasteful and complemented the décor of the room. A large gas fireplace and hearth was a focal point in the room.

The kitchen cupboards were of maple wood, and the countertops and island were granite. There were two Hotpoint wall ovens, a dishwasher, and a stove top. A small round kitchen table was in the corner by a bay window that could seat four people. The home wasn't extravagant, but it was immaculate, comfortable, and inviting. It was a place anyone could feel welcomed in.

From the photos, Doug could tell Donna came from a loving, close-knit family. There was one framed photograph, in particular, that caught his attention. It was a photo of Donna as a teenager in a graduation gown with a man, presumably her father, in a stylish suit and tie. He also saw a picture of Donna and Pete obviously on their wedding day. Donna was gorgeous, and Pete was a classy-looking guy as well. They looked so happy. There were lots of memories on those shelves, just like at his house. There were lots of similarities between this family and his, or so it seemed.

Looking at Donna's picture as a teen with her dad made him realize he had forgotten to call Taylor. Today had been so chaotic, he really hadn't had a chance to focus on his personal life. He had planned to take Taylor to dinner if she had time, but for sure, he had meant to check up on her to make sure she was okay. He definitely needed to do that right now. Tomorrow would be the first year anniversary of Cynthia's death.

"If you don't mind, Donna, I need to call Taylor for just a few minutes."

Doug pulled out his cell phone and dialed Taylor's cell phone.

"Hi, Dad."

"Hi, Taylor. I'm sorry I couldn't call sooner. I was tied up with a hostage situation."

"Yeah, I heard. Did everything come out all right?" Taylor asked.

"Not exactly. Donna Gifford's mother was one of the hostages inside the church."

"And?"

"She was shot, but she's going to be okay." Doug was quick to let her know that. Doug knew that Taylor thought the world of Donna and would be concerned about her.

"Oh, no! Is Donna okay?" Taylor asked.

"She's shaken up, as you can imagine. Donna was actually inside the church herself and held hostage."

"Did anyone get killed?" Taylor asked, getting to the point.

"No."

"So how many people got shot?"

"Just Stella. Donna's mother."

"How did that happen?"

"One of the hostage takers was attempting to shoot Donna, and her mother pushed her and took the bullet instead."

There was dead silence on the other end of the phone. Doug realized after he told her that that he probably shouldn't have. It was too close to home, especially at this time. It wasn't something Taylor needed to hear, so he tried to provide a distraction.

"Well, Donna is good, and her mom will be home from the hospital in a day or two, so I just brought Donna home and we're going to have a bite to eat and then I'm heading home."

"I'm glad everything at least turned out for her, Dad. Tell Donna I hope her mom gets along okay."

Doug didn't like the *at least*.

"Not all situations turn out bad like ours, Taylor."

"I understand, Dad. Listen, it sounds like you've had a long day and have your hands full right now, so I'll talk to you later."

"Are you okay, sweetie?"

"Yes, I'm fine. I'm really glad things came out a whole lot better for Donna than they did for us."

"Sweetie—"

"I'm fine, Dad, really. We'll talk later. Nightie."

"Nightie."

A smacking sound was heard from both ends as they kissed each other through the phone. It had always been their ritual.

After Doug hung up, he felt uneasy. He should have waited until tomorrow to call Taylor. He sensed she was troubled, and even more so because of events that played out with Donna's mother—as brief as those details were given to her.

"Doug, the pot pies just came out of the oven. Are you ready to eat?"

"Yes, I'm starving. I'll be right there."

Doug stared at his cell phone for a few seconds before putting it in his pocket. As the father of a young adult daughter, sometimes it was hard to know how far he should go to protect her. Taylor, Paul, and he had broken hearts over the loss of Cynthia. The way in which Cynthia had died was the hardest part to accept. They had all been through grieving classes and counseling.

A father never stops worrying about his children even when they become young adults. He knew Taylor so well, and he knew something was brewing inside of her . . . something that wasn't good.

CHAPTER 76

As soon as Doug walked into the kitchen, Donna picked up on the concerned look on his face.

"Is everything all right, Doug?"

"I'm not sure," he said.

"What is it? Is something wrong with Taylor?" she asked.

Doug then began to share his conversation with Taylor. Donna was aware of the many details of the Conrad crime. What she hadn't learned from the news media, she learned from Mitch Neubauer himself and Jean, their secretary. Then, of course, Donna was a participant when Quinton Reed had escaped on his trip to prison. She had been the one to actually shoot and kill Reed. She could fully appreciate what Taylor had been through.

"When I told Taylor about today's events and your mother getting shot, it was like a flashback for her, especially given the fact that tomorrow will be exactly one year since Cynthia was murdered. I should never have told Taylor that Stella was trying to protect you. Taylor has carried guilt feelings, believing that had she stayed in the woods that night, things might have played out differently and her mom might have been saved. In her mind, they would have been reunited and together, but the facts in the trial proved that Taylor would have been killed also. She just couldn't believe that. She always felt like there was more she could have done to save her mother."

"Her mom was probably trying to escape and do everything in her power to prevent Taylor from getting killed. Isn't that how I remember it?" asked Donna.

"Yes, she was. And here your mom was willing to die to save your life today, and I alluded to that, so Taylor is probably reliving that night in West Virginia and playing it out in her mind."

"So do you think you need to go get her and bring her home for a day or two?"

"She tried to assure me that she was okay, but I'm not too sure about that. She's never been one who needed to be pampered or patronized, but the circumstances are quite unique, and I'm not sure she realizes how fragile she really is just now."

As they ate their pot pies, they discussed today's events, compared notes, and Donna detailed for Doug what had been happening in the church when she got inside. He disclosed the note in the black truck with the name *Rabone* to Donna and how there might be a connection to the Mabel Bender murder case.

"Their attempt to rob the ladies of their purses was bizarre, to say the least," said Donna. "People hear about purse snatchers on the street, but they never hear of purse snatchers entering a place with so many women and grabbing all of them at once. They probably thought they would reap a lot for such little effort since they were mostly elderly women," theorized Donna.

Both Donna and Doug were deeply committed to their careers and solving crimes. Without realizing it, they had talked, shared ideas, and theorized about what happened today and in other cases they both had worked on that time got away from them. Doug looked at his watch. It was 11:20 p.m.

"Oops! It's been a long day, and we both need to get an early start tomorrow, so I need to get home. It was nice talking to you, Donna. I'm so glad Stella is going to be all right and things came out as well as they did, especially if these punks actually turn out to be murderers who target the elderly. God was certainly watching over all of you."

"He certainly was. Thanks so much for being there for me today, Doug. I appreciate it more than you will ever know."

"I'll be by at 8:15 in the morning to take you to get your car. Thanks for the dinner."

He gave her a wink, called out to Chunx, who by the way, had been sitting on the floor beside him most of the evening, and walked out to his car. Despite the stressful events of the day, it had almost been a welcomed distraction for him. He got to know Donna Gifford on a more personal level. She was professional and classy. Strong but warm. Concerned about others. She had good insight into life's dilemmas. He respected her opinions. She was family oriented. And pretty. Very pretty.

It was still too soon for him, but Donna Gifford was the kind of lady that he was attracted to. Both of their lives had been enriched by a loving spouse until they were widowed. Both felt a tremendous loss for what they once had. Perhaps in time—somewhere down the road—they could nurture their friendship.

CHAPTER 77

After Taylor's last afternoon class, she rushed back to her apartment and got her homework done for all of her classes. She typed a four-page paper on one of the stories in *The Canterbury Tales* for her Chaucer class along with a title page. After it came out of her printer, she proofread it one more time and then put it in a clear folder so that it was ready for submission tomorrow.

She then got on MapQuest and printed out a map and typed directions to a specific place outside Parkersburg, West Virginia. She reviewed them until they were memorized. She let her mind wander for at least fifteen minutes. Thoughts and images took her to a place she was afraid of going, and yet something inside was drawing her there. She needed to face her demons and fears head on. Despite all of her inward struggles this past year, somehow she needed to find peace. She had tried to bring this up to her dad and Paul when she last spoke with them over the phone. She wanted them to go on this journey with her—one last time. For her. But both were busy, involved, occupied with other things, and it seemed awkward to ask them to go along. She wasn't sure they would even understand or be able to relate to her needs. What would be a necessity for her could be a setback for them. So, no, she would be a big girl and go alone. Afterward, when she returned home, perhaps she could share her experience with them.

For right now, she needed to go to bed and get some rest. She would start her journey at 3:00 a.m., do what she needed to do, and return to Kent for her 2:30 Chaucer class.

Surprisingly, she fell asleep, which she didn't think she'd be able to do so early in the afternoon. She went into a dream mode. In this dream, she saw a very long road. There was nothing on either side of the road but trees and thicket. She kept walking on this road—it was long and straight and no one was on it but her. It didn't seem to lead to anywhere. Everything was so quiet and still, and then a light appeared on the road as it dead-ended. She couldn't tell what the source of the light was, but it was hovering over that one area of the road. It was a comforting light, warm and comforting. She walked in to the light and stopped, for there was no place she could go. She felt the warmth of the light, and then she awakened. She had never had a dream so strange and vague before. Minutes later she fell back into a deep sleep this time and didn't awaken until her alarm went off. It was now time to get dressed and begin her journey.

CHAPTER 78

Doug picked up Donna in time to retrieve her car in the church parking lot so she could make her 9:00 appointment with Jon Bates. He then drove to his office.

As soon as he walked in, Jean, his loyal secretary of ten years, handed him his phone messages, including one from Jon Bates. Doug filled Jean in on yesterday's events at Gospel Bible Church. She knew about some of it from what she learned on the local news channels. She didn't realize, however, that the woman shot was Donna's mother.

Doug then walked into Mitch Neubauer's office and sat down in one of his chairs. Mitch was just ending a phone conversation. Doug reviewed yesterday's events with him also and was going over what he knew about the Mabel Bender case that they had been working on together and how yesterday's so-called purse snatchers could actually be Mabel's killers.

"Hopefully, by now, those two guys have been interrogated and have spilled their guts. Looking at their mug shots on television this morning, they didn't look like cranial powers.

"Jean just handed me a phone message to call Jon Bates as soon as I got into the office. I'm hoping he's going to tell me they are our guys."

"Wouldn't that be something if they were?" remarked Mitch.

"My guess is, if they are, they've targeted others and may have a crime trail longer than any of us could imagine. Sometimes we underestimate guys like them, but they're street-smart."

"Yeah. Smart like a fox!" said Mitch.

Barnabus Johnson's grandmother's funeral was at 1:00 p.m., and Mitch and Doug had planned to attend the funeral out of respect for Barnabus. Ruby Johnson had raised Barnabus, and they knew he was having a hard time with his loss even though she had been in failing health for quite some time and her death was expected.

Flowers were sent to the funeral home, and food had been sent to Barnabus's home, so the final support would be to attend Ruby's funeral even though Doug and Mitch had never met her. Ruby Johnson had reared Barnabus from the time he was five years old. Neither Doug nor Mitch knew why, but Ruby had to be more like a mother to him than a grandmother.

Doug called Jon Bates but was told he was in a meeting and couldn't be disturbed. Doug would try back later. Both men worked through the morning and, at 12:30 p.m., left for the Anthony Funeral Home on Steese Road. The parking lot was full and overflowed to a parking lot across the street at the old Green Administration Building.

Doug and Mitch signed the guest book and followed the people standing in front of them into the room. Barnabus was standing by his grandmother's open casket. There was a long line of people waiting to speak to Barnabus, who was dressed in a black pin-striped suit, white shirt, and bright red tie. There were at least fifty floral arrangements and planters tiered around the casket in the front and some placed around the room. There were at least fifteen marines in uniform standing in line to speak to Barnabus. As they scanned the people, they were young and old, African Americans and whites, some crying, some laughing, but there was such a warm feeling in the room. Framed pictures of Ruby were placed on tables around the spacious room and a screen mounted on the wall was revealing the story of Ruby's life, displaying her many happy days through the slide presentation.

Mitch and Doug stood there and watched the entire slide show. Ruby's son, Barnabus's father, was a tall, strikingly handsome man. The lady with him was most likely Barnabus's mother. She was a petite lady. The majority of the pictures were of Ruby and her husband and Barnabus. Barnabus was a cute kid, and it was obvious from the photographs that the grandparents adored him. They had done many things with him. There were photos of them at the circus, on vacation trips at the ocean, sports events where Barnabus was in his team uniform. Then he was sitting with his grandfather at an Indians game, a Browns game, a Cavs game. There was his high school graduation picture and a military ceremony where he was graduating from boot camp from Parris Island. It was the story of a woman who had led a full life and was proud of her family, for you could see in every photograph the love they all had for one another.

It was quite refreshing and made Doug realize that all of these experiences with his family had molded and formed Barnabus into the man he was today.

When they made their way up to Barnabus, he thanked them so much for the sympathy card, the flowers and food, but especially for coming. His sincerity was genuine.

"Doug, I got a call from my grandmother's lawyer saying he wants to meet with me tomorrow morning at his firm regarding my grandmother's will. I knew she had one, but she never kept a copy in the house, nor would she ever talk to me about it. She didn't have all that much, so it shouldn't be too complicated. I'll probably need one more day away from the office, if you don't mind."

"No problem, Barnabus. Things got a little chaotic yesterday, but we may have solved one of our big cases. We've got you covered."

"Thanks."

They made their way to a pew midway back as the service was about to commence. A black minister stepped up to the podium, introduced himself, and led in a prayer. He read aloud Ruby's obituary, naming one surviving sister and one grandson, Barnabus.

A lady then stood up as an organ introduction began. She waited for her entrance. She began to sing, and her voice was sweet and melodic.

Jesus my Lord will love me forever,
From Him no power of evil can sever,
He gave His life to ransom my soul,
Now I belong to Him.

Once I was lost in sin's degradation,
Jesus came down to bring me salvation.
Lifted me up from sorrow and shame,
Now I belong to Him.

Now I belong to Jesus,
Jesus belongs to me,
Not for the years of time alone,
But for eternity.

After the song was over, Barnabus stepped up to the podium, holding several pages of typed notes. He took a deep breath and looked out at many friends, relatives, and even strangers. He smiled as though his heart was overflowing.

"Grandma would have been pleased to know so many of you came here today to bid her farewell."

He took another deep breath, and his countenance turned very somber.

"I have found that it is much easier to write a eulogy for someone you love and respect than it is to deliver it. As many of you know, I owe everything to my grandparents. Grandma was my mentor, my disciplinarian, my counselor, and my encourager.

"When I was five years old, my family was on the Ohio Turnpike. We were on our way to visit my mother's parents in Sandusky for Christmas. A large commercial eight-wheeler truck was passing us on our left but somehow lost control. It crashed into our car. Our car rolled several times. I was the only survivor. That is how I ended up living and growing up with Grandma and Grandpa Johnson.

"It was only after I became a young adult that I realized how that turned their lives and world upside down as well. They made the transition seem easy and welcoming, but I know it couldn't have been. Grandma was a seamstress who worked inside the home, and Grandpa was a tire builder at Firestone. Both of them worked very hard. They always told me they were going to raise me just like they did Reggie. That was my dad, their son.

"They insisted I study and get good grades. I got grounded if I slipped below a C, but they pretty much expected Bs or above. They allowed me to play sports and as you can see from the slides, they took me on some very nice summer vacations.

"As a young teen, I was expected to mow lawns and shovel snow for all of the old folks living in our neighborhood, and I was expected to do it for free. I was allowed to accept money only if middle-aged folk hired me.

"Serving my country was an expectation from the time I was young. My grandfather and all of his brothers served in the army or marines. My father served in the marines so, naturally, I proudly served in it as well. And, by the way, I thank many of my brothers for coming today.

"My grandparents were god-fearing people, and Grandma had me in Sunday school and church every Sunday whether I wanted to go or not. Truth of the matter, come Sunday morning, I wanted to sleep in, but that would never happen as long as I was living under her roof.

"Then, strangely enough, when I became a marine and was taken to many places around the world, I ended up going to a church service on Sundays every chance I got. Grandma wasn't watching, but I knew when I called home, she would ask me about that, and I couldn't lie to her.

"Grandma was proud of me. She bragged on me to all of her friends. She sent me care packages frequently and letters. Lots of letters.

"When Grandpa died, Grandma acted like she would be fine. She insisted I not worry about her and get on with my life. After my stint in the marines was over, she insisted I get enrolled in college and work on a degree. I got in on the GI Bill, but any extra expenses that were incurred, Grandma insisted on paying for. As I look back on that, I see what she was pulling. If she was paying and making sacrifices, she knew I would try harder to do my best. I didn't want to waste her hard-earned money nor disappoint her. She knew me so well. I probably would have done just enough to get by, but as it turned out, I made dean's list most of the semesters. I have Grandma to thank for that.

"She lived a modest life, but she was happy. Very happy. She loved so many people, and they loved her back. She reached out to help people whether they were black or white. It made no difference. She was color blind. Perhaps that's why so many white people are here today, and I don't mean to play a race card. She knew to look in to people's souls and not at skin color. She set that example for me too. We are *all* Americans, serving our country and our God.

"I will miss our many conversations. I will miss her warm hugs and encouragement, praise and love. I will miss her shoofly pie. I knew I wasn't going to get to keep her forever. That one day God would claim her, but she was there for a needy little five-year-old orphan when he needed her most. And I needed her until the day she left me. I hope I was a good grandson to her. I think I was.

"So today, I bid her good-bye, believing that someday I will see her again. Thank you for listening."

Barnabus sat down. It was quite a eulogy. It was very honoring to this lady who was his grandmother when really she was his surrogate mother. By having him continue to call them Grandma and Grandpa for all those years, it was obvious they never tried to take the place of his biological mother or father. They wanted him to keep both parents in his memory for life as well. That was pretty commendable.

The pastor returned to the podium and read a passage from the Bible, said some very kind words about Ruby, prayed, and concluded the funeral service for Ruby Johnson.

After walking by the casket for a final good-bye, Doug and Mitch patted Barnabus on the shoulder and quietly returned to Doug's car. Both men were quiet as they rode down the road, heading for the office.

Mitch broke the silence.

"You know, we spend so much time in our work tracking down bad people. Sometimes we lose sight of the Ruby Johnsons in this world. Don't you think, Doug?"

"Yeah, Mitch, we do. But what we do is make the world a safer place for nice people like Ruby Johnson to live in. We all have a job to do in life, a calling."

"I never knew all that about Barnabus, did you?" asked Mitch.

"Nope. It's no surprise now why he turned out so well. We all took the case of Andy Chandler hard. We're fathers so, naturally, we took that case very hard. I now understand why Barnabus, a young single guy had such compassion for Andy. Barnabus is a really good man. We're fortunate to have added him to our team."

"Yeah. He's been a good addition. So has Donna." With that last comment, Mitch looked over to watch Doug's face.

"Yes, you're right. I guess out of bad comes some good. When your life seems to be spinning out of control and you're being hurled through a vacuum, you have no peripheral vision for a while. It's only later that you can see things more clearly. It takes time, Mitch."

"I know, Doug. You're doing well, good buddy."

CHAPTER 79

Barnabus arrived at Parker, Leiby, Hanna, and Rasnick, LLC on South Main Street by his appointed time, 10:00 a.m. Yesterday had been one of the worst days of his life as he had to say good-bye to the most important person in his life. Yet in some ways, it was a good day. At least twenty people he didn't even know stopped by the funeral home to pay final homage to his grandmother before she was laid to rest. They all had a story to tell of how his grandmother had helped them in a time of need. These were stories he had never heard before. Many of these people had tears in their eyes as they shared their story. Barnabus couldn't help but believe that while Grandma was never rich in this life, her rewards would surely be many in her new one.

Grandma always seemed to have what she wanted. She lived comfortably, and he never heard her yearn for things that were out of her financial reach, yet he wished he could have done more for her in this life.

He turned the doorknob to suite 402, identified himself to the receptionist, and asked to see Mr. John Rasnick. He took a seat in the reception area, and in less than five minutes, Mr. Rasnick came out, greeted him warmly, and led him to a conference room.

"I'm very sorry for your loss, Barnabus. I've known your grandparents for over twenty years. They were both fine people.

"Your grandmother called me about a month ago. She knew she didn't have long to live. She wanted to review with me the instructions she and your grandfather had set up in 1991. I visited her in your home, and we went through her will line by line. She was very fastidious about every detail. She also handed me a letter that she had handwritten some time back and wanted me to give it to you before I show you her will."

With that Mr. Rasnick handed Barnabus a sealed envelope with his name on it and in his grandmother's handwriting. Barnabus broke the seal and began to read:

My beloved Barnabus,

Your grandfather and I never realized that we would become parents of a five-year-old when we were in our late forties. The accident and death of our Reggie and his beautiful wife came as a terrible shock, and the loss was more than we could almost bear, but the good Lord got us through it. He did it by giving *you* to us to rear.

Milton and I were comfortable financially and knew we would be able to support you. Your parents, to our surprise, had a sizable life insurance policy that came through upon their deaths. After their burial costs, we were able to put some of it into a special bank account for you solely. Then we learned that you were entitled to social security benefits because of your folks having died and that money began arriving in the mail.

We didn't believe in suing, but the trucking company gave us $300,000 for our loss. We signed papers stating we accepted the amount and could not attempt to sue them at a later date. The weather was awful the day of the accident, and the turnpike that night was icy. The accident was just that—an accident. That $300,000 was not something we ever expected to get. So with the $300,000 and the remainder of your parents' life insurance policy, Milton and I spoke with a financial consultant from Raymond James and asked him to invest money for you.

Mr. Cavalena has had charge over your money since you were five. He has taken a safe, conservative approach and only on a few occasions taken some high risks that proved to be lucrative moves. Mr. Rasnick has been in contact with Mr. Cavalena and will provide for you an update on the amount.

Milton and I kept this information from you for all of these years. It was purposeful.

Money has brought down many good people, and we didn't want that to happen to you. Sometimes people lose their incentive to work and lead useful, productive lives. They contribute nothing to society. We wanted you to learn to work for things you wanted so that you would appreciate them when you finally earned them. We wanted you to take nothing for granted.

We wanted you to grow up living a normal childhood. You had no more than any other kid you played with. We watched you get excited when you finally got something you had longed to have for months.

We wanted you to succeed at everything through hard work and effort so that you felt pride in your accomplishments. We didn't want you to lose incentive or to think you could buy your way to success.

We felt you would appreciate the money more once you got older and were more mature. Boy toys are out of your system by now, and the money is now available for purchasing a house or a car or for getting married and getting a financial start for raising children. (And, by the way, I always liked Serena Billings. She's a beautiful young lady who would be perfect for you, and I'm sure she has her eye on you. Just a thought.)

Barnabus couldn't help but smile at that. Grandma was always trying to set him up, and she was getting the last say in.

When you read the will, I know you will be pleasantly surprised as was I, actually. Milton and I tried to do our best by you, Barnabus, and I know that we succeeded. You are such a good boy who made us so proud. You never gave us an ounce of trouble but gave us bundles of joy and love. Your mom and dad would have been so pleased to see how you turned out too.

I can do no more for you, my dear grandson, so I trust that you will continue to fulfill the goals and dreams you had before today and before the reading of the will. Serve society well and reach out to help others who are struggling and in need. You should be financially secure for the rest of your life *if* you live a prudent life. I put you on your honor, for I know you are an honorable man.

All my love,
Grandma Ruby

Barnabus looked up from the letter and was stunned by the contents. He had no idea about his parents' life insurance policy or the settlement with the trucking company.

Mr. Rasnick handed him the will, and he watched closely as Barnabus began to read it. Barnabus got to the part that said he had just inherited over 1.5 million dollars, and he began to literally sob. The information was too overwhelming for him. It was mind-boggling and unfathomable.

John Rasnick quietly slipped out of the room and let Barnabus have some time to process the news.

"I'll be back in about ten minutes. Take your time to reread and collect yourself, and then we'll proceed. There's a carafe of hot coffee on the credenza. Help yourself."

CHAPTER 80

Greg Marshall and Chase Manning had been high school buddies, playing football together for all four years. They had remained friends since the ninth grade when they had first met in Mr. Greene's Algebra 1 class. The years had come and gone and taken them in different directions, but that never deterred them from getting together for sports events or deer hunting, which were two of their favorite pastimes.

Greg drove over to Chase's house around 4:00 a.m. to pick up Chase and load up his deer equipment and .243 Winchester rifle in the back of his truck. They took turns driving, and it just happened to be Greg's turn to drive this time. They hunted deer in the same location each time for several reasons: the population of the deer was pretty heavy in this area and a permanent deer blind was built in a tree so that one of them didn't have to set theirs up and it saved time. It was sturdy and bigger than most. Lots of hunters knew about it. Everyone living in the area knew it had been built years ago by Brady Randolph's family. Everyone also knew that Brady Randolph had been murdered there in the past year, and that sort of hindered other hunters from going there. Their chance of getting to use it today was great. Greg and Chase tossed a coin to see who would get it today, and Chase won. Greg would drive down a path through the wood and drop Chase off. He would then drive about seven-tenths of a mile farther down the road and set up his own deer blind. They had agreed to hunt until about noon and then call it quits unless one of them actually got a deer. Then they would gut it in the wood, load it on the truck, and take it to the butcher at Blevins Meat

Packing company who would have deer steaks and deer burgers ready to be picked up two days later.

Both young men had their cell phones on so if either had a problem or got a deer, he could call the other for assistance. They would keep their phones on vibration, naturally.

As Chase got out of the truck, the truck lights lit up the shed that had also been there for years. It was a bit eerie as both young men knew this was not only the place where Brady Randolph's body was found crumpled in the back of his flatbed but where the Conrad woman had been held hostage and ultimately murdered on the path just beyond Brady's deer blind. All the locals knew this, but of course, it had been big national news that had occurred in their hometown. As Chase stepped out of the truck, he tried not to really look at the shed.

"Let's hope it's our lucky day, and we both get a deer," Chase said softly.

"Stay safe, comrade. I'll be back to pick you up around noon unless anything changes," said Greg. Greg turned his truck around in the one open area and quietly drove back up the path to which he had come.

Chase turned on his flashlight and made his way down the path as quickly and quietly as he could so as not to forewarn the deer. The path was dark and fairly narrow.

When Chase got situated in the deer blind, he found a comfortable position for his six-foot-four-inch frame. He was a big guy with long legs, so it was hard to squeeze into the blind, even this blind that had been hand built and was bigger than most. He surveyed his surroundings once his eyes adjusted to the dark. Early dawn and at dusk were the best times to get a deer. Chase had high hopes for today. It was going to be his lucky day. He had no idea what was in store for him.

CHAPTER 81

She was getting closer now. A frightening, bad feeling was coming over her. At least this time she was driving and not locked in the trunk of Kevin Reed's car. Taylor began to relive every minute of that evening from the time she had voluntarily chosen to meet Kevin a.k.a. Tim Smith at his car and ended up drugged, subdued, and later chloroformed and taken out of Ohio to West Virginia.

When she was finally assisted out of his trunk, it was quite dark. She saw a glimpse of a shed and then heard gunfire. That was when Kevin Reed gave her his car keys and told her to go for help as quickly as she could. She did. Later she learned that the gunfire she heard was Quinton Reed killing her mother in the woods. Later, she learned many details about the crime from the West Virginia police, the local coroner, and from the prosecutors at Quinton Reed's trial.

She knew her mom had been raped and then managed to escape the shed shortly afterward. She followed a path that led into the woods, hoping to hide and eventually escape, but the short path really dead-ended, leading to nowhere. It was on this path that her mother was shot in the back—shot in cold blood and died alone.

And yet she herself had been right there minutes before. Had she known her mother was in the woods, she never would have left. She would have tried to help her mother fight Quinton Reed off, something. Instead, she fled for help that would come much too late.

Taylor passed the farmhouse that she had gone up to, begging for them to let her in. They wouldn't, but they did call the police as she had requested. Now she knew she was a mile or so away from the hidden path that led down to the shed.

She looked at the clock in her car. It was 5:45 a.m. Good. It would still be dark, and she could play through the events of that night. This would be very emotional for her, but she needed to do it. She wanted to lie down on the very spot that her mother had taken her final breath. She wanted to feel close to her. To say she was sorry she didn't try to help but that she really didn't know she was there. She knew she was probably torturing herself, but she felt compelled to play this out. In her own strange way, she needed one last moment to sense her mother's spirit, to feel close to her. To apologize for not having done more.

So, now, here she was going down this infamous path that led her to the very worst day of her life.

CHAPTER 82

There before her was the shed. She closed her eyes as she remained in the car and whispered a prayer—for her emotional recovery, for her brother's, and especially for her father's. She prayed and asked God to hug her mother for her.

It was time to reenact that night. There was no full moon as there had been the night her mom died, but there was part of a moon that wasn't able to shed even a glimmer on the path. Taylor always kept a flashlight in her car and turned it on as she stepped out of her car. It would have to be her sole light source. She didn't want to keep her car lights on, for she didn't want the possibility of being spotted by any passing cars up on the road. She needed to be alone and draw no attention to herself.

She walked over to the shed. Of course the door was bolted shut and there was a sign posted on the door: No Trespassing. Her hands went up and down the door. She walked around all sides of the shed, searching for any possible means of escape, but there weren't any. There was a very tiny vent at the bottom, but it was so small, no human could have passed through it. Perhaps her mom could have at least gotten a little more air.

Taylor returned to the front door, standing directly in front of it. She turned off her flashlight to make her experience as authentic to her mother's as possible. She looked out and found the path that her mother took and began to run down it. She would run until the path ended.

CHAPTER 83

Chase heard a car coming down the path as cinders hit its hubcaps and wheel wells. He was surely hoping it wasn't another deer hunter invading his territory. The car lights went out, and he heard a car door slam although he was too far away to actually see anything. He feared whoever was here would make enough noise to scare the deer if there were any around.

He saw a faint light, which was moving. While he couldn't actually see through the woods quite that far, it looked like someone was snooping around the shed, but who in the world would be doing that at this crazy hour?

He thought he would be alone this morning. He wanted to be alone and have the whole area to himself. The last thing he needed was company. Since Greg hadn't called him, he knew the vehicle wouldn't be his, but he was the only person who knew where Chase was right now.

Chase decided to remain as quiet as possible. He didn't want to give away his location or his presence. He didn't move a muscle but remained vigilant. His rifle was in shooting position while his curiosity was piqued. If a crime hadn't been committed here in the past year, Chase probably wouldn't have felt spooked, but his life experiences had taught him to be prepared for anything when you least expect it. However, he had also been trained by some great deer hunters to never shoot unless you see the target and know exactly what you're shooting.

Then he heard thumping sounds, sounds like someone or something running in his direction. Had the car stirred up a deer? Was he lucky enough to have it run toward him rather than away from him? He waited.

He was ready to take the shot, but he *must* see the target first. His rifle was aimed right on the path. The sound of running was coming closer and closer.

As the object was almost directly passing his tree, Chase could tell it was human. He knew immediately it would not be a deer hunter making that loud of noise, for he would surely know to take quiet, slow steps. Even more puzzling to him was that the footsteps sounded like those of a female. What would a woman be doing out here alone and running like that in the dark? Was she being pursued by someone? Was she afraid of something or someone? Was she trying to hide? He was starting to get the creeps.

He continued to follow the sound of the footsteps until they stopped. He knew the path ended about twenty yards beyond him. Things are so quiet in the woods in the early hours that one can hear acoustically every sound that's made from even far distances.

Chase sat still and just listened. Then he heard a female's voice. She seemed to be on the ground. She was sobbing. He didn't even have to strain to hear her.

"Oh, Mom. I'm here! A year later, but I'm here. I'm so sorry. Forgive me. I didn't know you were here or I might have been able to save your life. I wouldn't have run away. I would have run into the woods to help you. It made no sense what he did. Why? Why did he take your life? You didn't do anything to him. It's not fair!

"I miss you so much, Mom. I'm trying to move on with my life, but it's so hard. I needed to talk to you one more time. I need to feel your presence here—your spirit. I want to feel what *you* felt. I need to reconcile my guilt, my regrets. I need to face my fears. I need to ask God why He allowed this to happen? I demand an answer—out here . . . alone. From God. I would have given up my life for you, Mom, and I'm sure you would have done the same for me."

Chase could hear every word the girl was saying, and then he realized who she was. It was the Conrad woman's daughter although he couldn't remember her name from the news. He could remember Cynthia's name and her detective husband, Doug, but not the two kids' names. There are so many famous criminal cases that get so much national attention that people can remember the names and their cases: Sam Shepard, Charles Manson, Susan Smith, Jeffrey Dahmer, O. J. Simpson, Lacy Peterson,

Casey Anthony, the Conrad murder, and especially that one since it happened right here in their hometown no more than a year ago.

Chase's own mother had been murdered during a robbery seven years ago while working at their family business. He knew what this girl was feeling, and he felt guilty that he was an innocent eavesdropper into her most private and vulnerable moment. But actually, it wasn't safe for her to be in this woods right now. No telling how many deer hunters were out here besides him or how many shoot at any sound, throwing all hunting rules to the wind.

Chase wasn't quite sure what he should do. He could remain anonymous and hope eventually she returns to her car and drives away. She didn't seem like she was in any condition to do that. What if she came here to kill herself? She confessed she was guilt ridden.

Perhaps he could identify himself to her, tell her his story and console her. Maybe this wasn't a chance meeting but a God-given one. Divine intervention, as Chase liked to think of it.

Chase decided to come down from the deer blind and identify himself so she'd know he was there. He didn't want to scare her. He quietly climbed down, bringing his rifle with him in case he wasn't able to return to the blind and resume his hunting. He was wearing his camouflage deer suit and was getting ready to lean his rifle against the tree when Taylor heard him and saw his shadow close by. She nervously reached for her flashlight, saw this huge man with a rifle, panicked, and went into attack mode. She would be fighting for her life, just like her mother.

Chase didn't see it coming at first, but she screamed out just as she landed a hard kick to his leg and hit him in the face with her fist. A sucker punch? This girl sucker punched him? He could hardly believe it. She was in such a rage he had no time to identify himself to her or present a peace pipe. He had to ward off her blows. He tried to grab her wild, flailing arms, but she was so fast, he had never been up against a foe who fought this way. She was like a raging tiger. He had had combat training in the military, but his goal was to overpower her but not hurt her. She had been through enough already *if* she was the Conrad girl.

Just then she scratched his face all the way down both cheeks. He tried to grab on to her wrists when she suddenly kicked him in the groin. He dropped to his knees in excruciating pain.

"I'm a deer hunter," he called out. "I'm not going to hurt you. I promise. Please calm down. Stop!" Chase yelled out. It was, however, as though she never even heard him.

His camouflaged vest and jacket was thick, so she really didn't hurt him too badly when she hit him in the chest, but then she latched on to his ungloved hands with her teeth and wouldn't let go. She bit him so deeply that blood was dripping from his hand.

"My name is Chase Manning. I'm twenty-five years old and I over—"

She bit his other hand as he struggled to push her away. He had had enough. He was taking a brutal beating from her. He had combat training, so he knew how to get her under control. He resisted hurting her, but he had to get the upper hand on her or she'd kill him. His bulky hunting gear made things a little more difficult.

She continued to kick him in the shins as he tried to turn her body around and get dominance over her. He knew there would be several ways he could do that. The best way would be to interrupt her flow of oxygen and another would be to cut off her flow of blood. Either of these were risky moves, but when they work, they are fight enders.

Chase managed to bring his right arm around her throat. The crook in his elbow was sitting right against her trachea. He rested the elbow of his left arm against her opposite shoulder and using his right hand grabbed her opposite bicep. He now had a hard, firm grip on her.

He then reached down with his nondominant hand and grabbed the back of her head, pushing it down into his arm. He flexed his forearm and his right bicep so that he was squeezing both sides of her neck. In less than fifteen seconds, she'd passed out.

Chase's heart was pounding, but before she regained consciousness, he needed to call for help. He called Greg and hoped he would answer spontaneously. Thankfully, he did.

"Greg, I need help. Call the police and get an ambulance here quickly. I'm okay. But there's a girl out here who is wild and having a meltdown. I'm serious. Call and come help me."

"Okay" was all Greg had time to say before his friend hung up his cell.

Greg never asked any questions. While he didn't know the circumstances, he knew Chase met up with some kind of trouble and that this wasn't a joke. He could hear the trouble in his voice. He called 911, gave them directions, and of course, everyone in the area was quite aware of this particular location, and Greg hung up, grabbed his rifle, and got in the car, heading for Chase.

CHAPTER 84

Chase knew that if he got his timing wrong and maintained his hold past the point of consciousness, he could kill her. This was called the sleeper hold. When the girl passed out, Chase had her in a position that would not allow her to hit or kick him again.

Chase was so afraid he may have seriously hurt her. He could hear the sirens getting closer, and he knew this scenario wasn't going to look good when the police would arrive. What if he wasn't believed and he became a suspect of an assault?

A truck with its bright lights came barreling down the path. Chase knew it was Greg and was relieved when Greg had a bright flashlight on and was sprinting into the woods, full speed ahead, with rifle in hand.

Just then the girl came to and saw yet another guy with a rifle coming toward her. She let out a scream and once again began fighting his tight grip on her. She gave him a head butt that almost made him pass out. His nose was bleeding profusely. She was screaming at the top of her lungs.

"What in the heck is going on here, Chase? Who is she?"

"I think she's the Conrad girl."

"The Conrad girl? Why would she be here and at this time of morning?"

"I think I know, but right now just help me get her under control!" said Chase.

Two police cars and the paramedics were speeding down the path with lights flashing. The police had their guns drawn as they were running on the path, following the sounds of the screams.

"My name is Chase Manning, and my friend with me is Greg Marshall. We were deer hunting when this girl—I believe she's the Conrad girl—showed up. She's having some sort of emotional breakdown, I think."

"Release her now," said the deputy with his gun pointed at all three. The other deputies were standing beside him with their guns pointed also.

As soon as he released her, Taylor got up and started attacking Chase and Greg, kicking them and hitting them.

Several police officers grabbed Taylor to get her under control, but she began to scream and attack them.

"No! No! You're all trying to kill me. You killed my mom, and now you're trying to kill me. Dad! Dad! I need your help!"

The one officer instructed the paramedics to assist them so she could be restrained and taken to the nearest hospital. The police were almost certain she was indeed the Conrad girl even though it was dark out there and they couldn't make a clear identification of her.

Taylor was strapped in a gurney with restraints and was still resisting and out of control. She was in the ambulance and on her way to Camden-Clark Memorial Hospital.

CHAPTER 85

By now Chase's left eye was nearly swollen shut and blackened. His nose and both hands were bleeding. It was obvious to all of the deputies that Chase had borne the worst part of the fight with this female. He was a big guy, and the girl was perhaps five-feet-five and thin. The guy looked like he could have ripped the girl into pieces, so either he was a wussy, which most deer hunters in this area weren't or he was a perfect gentleman. The forthcoming investigation would give them their answers.

"Until we know what's going on here, we're going to handcuff you and take you downtown."

The one deputy looked at Chase's wounds and said, "We'll take you to the emergency room and get you assessed, treated, and cleaned up first. We can hear your story on the way to the hospital."

Greg was being handcuffed and put in the other deputy's car. Greg heard him tell the deputy, "I'm the one who called you, guys, for help."

"Take care, Chase. I'm sure they'll get this sorted out for us soon."

Chase felt sorry for Greg because he really had no idea what had happened. This hunting excursion would certainly be one they'd both remember for a very long time.

On the way to the hospital, Chase told the deputies his story. He identified himself, and once they knew he was the son of the owner of Manning's Jewelers, they knew he was most likely telling the truth. After all, as bizarre as this story was, truth is often stranger than fiction, and they had been deputies long enough to have seen that played out.

The deputies remembered when Manning's Jewelers was robbed and Mrs. Manning had been murdered. They weren't working that case, but they knew the guys who were. It was an awful tragedy that had received a lot of publicity. The Mannings were good people. This son was in high school when his mother had been murdered, so they knew Chase's story was true. It was all making sense. The officer who wasn't driving the squad car called downtown. He made some inquiries and learned that today was the first year anniversary of Cynthia Conrad's murder. It was a date that had significance for this young woman.

Greg Marshall would still be interrogated at the station to see if their stories matched, but they would make the call, enter a report quickly, and see that Greg Marshall would be treated with respect and released.

All the evidence supported Chase's story. The car by the shed was registered to Taylor Conrad, and the purse sitting on the passenger's seat contained her driver's license, clearly identifying her.

These two deer hunters just happened to be at this particular place for a reason. It may have been a good thing for this girl but scary for the guys.

CHAPTER 86

Chase was being treated in the emergency room with the officers right in the room with him. They had to cauterize his nose to stop the bleeding, but at least his nose hadn't been broken. They cleaned the scratches on his cheeks and applied an antibiotic salve on them. The wounds of greatest concern were the deep bites on both of his hands. Human bites can be quite serious if left unattended.

The ER doc numbed the bites with lidocaine and then thoroughly cleaned and examined the wounds for joint space violation and tendon injury. Skin breaks from human bites increase the risk of infection. He squirted copious amounts of saline into the wound. A small amount of antiseptic solution was again added before rinsing the wounds and skin with saline. Since Chase hadn't had a tetanus booster shot within the past five years, he was going to require one now. There was some swelling, redness, and bruising around the bites, but the pain was subsiding. There didn't seem to be a concern about transmission of HIV so a blood test wasn't ordered. The doctor wrote out a prescription for Augmentin, an antibiotic, to prevent infection and instructed him to take it as directed for the full course.

He then gave Chase a list of warning signs of infection: worse swelling at the wound areas, fever, pus drainage, or red streaking up his arms in the next day or two. If he saw thin red streaks running up his arms, it would confirm infection, and he would be suffering from lymphangitis, which put in layman terms was blood poisoning, whereupon he would need to immediately return to the ER or see his family practitioner. The physician felt his bite wounds would be best left open and really didn't expect there to be a continued problem.

Now that he had time to process this whole thing, it seemed more like he had just had an encounter with a lioness rather than a sweet, mourning young lady who missed her mother. And yet, if anyone knew the anger that is pent up inside when a parent is murdered, he did. He went through that too, but it had been seven years ago, and time made a difference for him. Nevertheless, the memory of his mother's death was still very painful.

CHAPTER 87

As soon as Taylor arrived in the ER, she continued her crying and screaming. By then everyone knew who she was and what had happened. She was given a shot of lorazepam (one milligram, intramuscular) to calm her and get her stabilized. A complete drug screen was ordered along with a blood test and a CT scan to eliminate any unknown head injuries that may have contributed to her behavior. The treating staff was also made aware that this was the first anniversary of her mother's murder.

After the work up was completed and they had to wait for the test results, Taylor was taken to the psychiatric floor. Once on the floor, she was given ten milligrams Lexopro, an anxiety medicine. It would take fourteen days to take effect, but she definitely needed to get started on that.

The resident psychiatrist spoke with Taylor in an effort to assess her condition. If the shot of lorazepam wore off and she was still somewhat unstable, Dr. Elkins would then give her the meds in a pill form every eight hours as needed for anxiety. If she was highly out of control, she would need another shot as it got quicker results. Tomorrow morning she would be visited by a psychiatrist who would determine if this was a temporary meltdown due to the circumstances, or if she would need extensive and continuous counseling and therapy.

Several hours later, Dr. Elkins checked on Taylor and found her at rest and sleeping. She studied Taylor's now peaceful face and tried to imagine all that this young girl had been through. She felt so sorry for her. She couldn't imagine what it would be like to have your mother murdered and then to be kidnapped yourself and put in a car trunk and taken across state lines. And then the murderer attempts to kill you and you witness him being murdered right in front of you. In fact, his dead body falls on top of yours. How traumatic would that be for a teen?

Taylor's father needed to be notified. The resident was told that the police were calling Mr. Conrad. It would be a call that no father would want to get. After all, he had been through a lot himself. The entire family had. Hopefully, this would just be a temporary setback for his daughter. Everyone on the floor was wishing that for her.

CHAPTER **88**

Doug arrived in his office early. He had some paperwork to do, and then he was going to try to get hold of Jon Bates. They had been playing phone tag for the past twenty-four hours. Bates and his SWAT team were, no doubt, interviewing all of yesterday's hostages separately, so he knew the commander wasn't just sitting around doing nothing. He suspected Bates was going to fill him in on the interrogations of the two hostage takers and any links to Doug's case.

An hour later he put the call in to Bates and got hold of him.

"Doug, we have some interesting breaks with those two guys that I think you will find pretty fascinating.

"We now know their true identities: Eddie Flatt and Bobby Forwark. Have you ever heard of them?"

"No, should I?"

"Not really. They have been flying under the radar like we thought. So far we haven't been able to find any priors on either of them. They move from state to state, pay cash for everything so there's no paper trail. They were relying on that for their security.

"Eddie Flatt has been tight-lipped with us, but Bobby Forwark has been a different story. Eddie was read his Miranda right at the church before we took him to the hospital. Of course, he wanted to be lawyered up. We had to wait for Forwark to wake up at the hospital, and then we read him his Miranda rights. He was willing to talk before his lawyer arrived.

"Bobby admitted that they were both unemployed and had been since they got out of high school. Not willing to live on the government's dollar, they would do odd jobs for people for pickup money. He mentioned helping the elderly with yard work or putting on a roof. They were willing to do 'an honest day's worth of labor and not rely on handouts.'

"Eddie clammed up when we asked him about the unusual note on the seat of his truck. When we mentioned the name *Rabone* and Mabel Bender, he knew we had him. We were able to obtain where they were temporarily living, so we got a search warrant. What do you think we found in their room? Fifty thousand dollars in one bag and fifteen thousand dollars in another. We are tracing the money now, but we're almost certain it will be traced to Mabel Bender's bank and Lois Lawrence's bank. There was a lot more cash found in the room that neither man could explain where it came from.

"Several hours later, Bobby Forwark asked to talk to us and wanted to work a deal. I think we have enough evidence now to charge them with two murders, along with attempted murder of Stella LaMarre, and the robbery of twenty-five ladies.

"We feel confident that if we keep looking at some of our unsolved cold cases from past years, the trail may lead to them as well. Their MO is easy to track. Authorities from nearby states are interested in interviewing these two guys, and well, their future doesn't look too favorable.

"That's all we have so far, but you may want to give Dan Bender a call and update him on what we've found regarding his mother's case. Let him know that one of our officers will stop by in several days and provide him with information if we can prove beyond any reasonable doubt that these two guys are our men.

"Oh, and by the way, Chris Lambert can put Bobby Forwark at Lois Lawrence's house the day before she was found murdered. So we are trying to connect the dots and work on a confession.

"You were right, Doug. These guys were far more than just purse snatchers. And, by the way, I'll be stopping by the hospital sometime today to interview Stella LaMarre. My secretary called Akron General this morning and learned that Stella was alert and could talk to us now. After all the years we used to work together, Doug, we still make a good team. Well, I need to get busy. Talk to you later."

"Thanks for the update, Jon. If I uncover anything, I'll give you a call."

As soon as Doug hung up, he called Flowers by Dick to see if his bouquet of red roses was ready to be picked up. He had put his order in yesterday. It was. He left the office, picked up the flowers, and drove to Greenlawn Cemetery. It's strange, but it matters not how many thousands of flat gravestones are on the premises, one never forgets where his loved one lies. He walked up a slight grade near three huge oak trees that were planted in a straight row. Between the second and third oak was Cynthia's grave.

He looked around and saw no one, not even a groundskeeper. He studied Cynthia's gravestone with her name and the date of her birth, a dash, and the date of her death. He thought about the dash that represented the story of her life—their life together. It was such a happy life until it was abruptly snatched from her, and from him. It was exactly one year to the day that Cynthia had died. It seemed like a hundred years ago. This had been a very lonely year for him. He had been forced to make many adjustments. He hadn't been successful with some of them. So many memories came rushing to his mind. Tears rolled down his cheeks as he placed the beautiful roses on her grave. He didn't want to leave, but the longer he stayed, the more painful it was for him. This was a nightmare that was never going to go away. Never.

He whispered, "I love you, Cynthia. I always will," and then turned reluctantly and walked to his car.

As soon as he started the car up, his cell phone began to ring. It was an out-of-state call.

CHAPTER 89

"Doug Conrad."

"Mr. Conrad, this is the Parkersburg, West Virginia Police Department calling. I'm Lt. Russ Sanders."

"Yes, Lieutenant. Is something wrong?" Doug knew there was, or they wouldn't be calling.

"I'm afraid your daughter, Taylor, is at the Camden-Clark Memorial Hospital right now. In the psychiatric ward. We believe she returned to the place her mother died and had some kind of an emotional meltdown. Apparently, two deer hunters found her in the woods and called for help. She's being treated, but I think you need to get here, sir."

"I'm on my way, Lieutenant. Thanks for letting me know."

Doug Conrad aimed his car for home to pack a small suitcase and make a call to his office and to Mitch. He then called his best friend and pastor, Jim Pascoe, who volunteered to come along, but Doug declined his offer. Last, he called Paul who didn't answer his phone, so Doug left a message: "I don't expect you to come, Paul. I just wanted you to know what happened and where I'll be." He then repeated what Lieutenant Sanders told him. "I'll keep you abreast of Taylor's condition once I get there. You were right. I think Taylor was trying to reach out to us with her phone calls. I should have responded to her sooner."

Doug rushed home, packed some toiletries, socks, two shirts, trousers, jocks, and an extra pair of shoes. He returned to his car, set the GPS, and stopped at GetGo to gas up before pulling onto the highway heading for Parkersburg. He would be there short of two hours. He would have a lot to process on his way there.

Doug felt guilty that he didn't react differently to Taylor when she called or hadn't picked up on her emotional need yesterday. He was involved in a crisis at the time she called, but he could have asked Holly Pascoe, their pastor's wife and Taylor's surrogate mother, to call her.

This past year had been hard on their family but probably hardest on his two children, and especially hard on Taylor. She had such a close relationship with her mother. She had just turned twenty when her mom was murdered; she herself was kidnapped and almost killed not once but three times, went through a grueling trial, and saw the murderer who had escaped custody get killed right in front of her. Geez! And we thought she was over all of this in one year? She had gone through lots of counseling—they all had—but she felt she was ready to end it and move on. She was doing well in school and leading an active social life although he didn't think she had been dating at all. After the ruse Kevin Reed, alias Tim Smith, had pulled on her, almost costing her her life, her level of trust in men probably plummeted to zero. Doug was okay with that as she needed to focus on her studies and work on her emotional recovery. Time would take care of the dating situation.

Doug knew the anniversary date of Cynthia's death prompted Taylor's actions and reaction. Hopefully, counselors and the family support can move her forward and get her through this new hurdle without too much collateral damage. Today certainly had a major effect on him too, so he could expect Taylor would struggle with it as well. God never said life would be easy, but He did say He would be "our refuge and strength, a very present help in trouble." And "many are the afflictions of the righteous, but the Lord delivers him out of them all." Lots of Bible verses were coming to Doug, and they gave him assurances that God would get every one of the Conrads through this tragedy—and in one piece!

CHAPTER 90

Doug walked up to the information desk at Camden and inquired where to find the psychiatric floor. Mrs. Johnston had worked behind that desk for nearly twenty-three years and knew almost everything there was about the hospital. She knew when there were famous or infamous patients admitted to Camden and their room numbers. She was aware of any famous visitors that came through the front doors to visit someone. She knew about exciting cases that came in. She knew details of the tragedies and trauma cases that came through the ER minutes after they arrived. She also knew every doctor, nurse, all the clerical and janitorial staff, and she knew everyone working in security. Nothing got past Mrs. Johnston. She was a wealth of knowledge.

As soon as she saw Doug Conrad walk in, she recognized him. She knew Taylor Conrad had been admitted to the psychiatric floor early this morning. She knew who she was—didn't everyone? So she was expecting the famous Doug Conrad to show up some time today.

Doug followed her directions to the hallway that would put him on the right elevator for going up to the fourth floor. As soon as the elevator doors opened, he followed the sign that pointed to a desk that had solid double doors behind it. He knew those doors would be locked from both sides. No one gets in or out without the permission of a floor supervisor. Once again the supervisor recognized Doug and had even been expecting him.

The lady behind the desk asked him to wait while she made a call granting permission for his entrance into the ward. She explained that Taylor's physician wanted to speak to him before he visited with his daughter. Contact was made, and the lady behind the desk pushed a button, and only one door opened.

"Dr. Lynn Felderman will meet you at the nurse's station straight ahead, Mr. Conrad. She'll be easy to find. She has long beautiful red hair."

Indeed she was easy to identify. Dr. Felderman was on the phone talking to the hospital pharmacist from the sound of the conversation. She held a finger up to him indicating she would be free in a minute.

In a minute or so, she hung the phone up and stepped out of the nurse's station to greet Doug. She had a broad smile, beautiful teeth, a cute dimple, and lovely red hair.

"It's very nice to meet you, Mr. Conrad, although I'm sorry it's under these circumstances. Let's walk down the hallway to one of our private conference rooms where we can discuss what's going on with Taylor."

"Okay" was all Doug could think to say.

The conference room was a rather small room. There was a draped window that provided natural light. There were four beautifully upholstered high-back chairs that were facing one another. Dr. Felderman sat in one chair and pointed to the chair directly across from her. Doug sat down.

"Let me say right from the start that I believe that what has happened to your daughter is a temporary problem. She is going to get better, and it will not be a long-term recovery. That is my professional opinion. I have been wrong before, but I don't think I will be proven wrong this time. I say that because everyone reacts to things differently. Where human emotion is concerned, there are no cookie cutters. Few people are the perfect textbook cases. That's what I'm trying to get across here. Psychiatry isn't an exact science.

"Your daughter went to the wooded area where her mother was murdered. Reexperiencing takes the form of recurrent recollections of the event. So, while there, she had a flashback or reactivity upon exposure to a traumatic cue.

"By seeing the spot where her mom was shot, she had an adverse emotional and psychological consequence of short-term duration brought on, as I said, by the environment she placed herself in.

"She felt guilty that she was there that tragic night, left, fleeing for help. Psychological devastation experienced by survivors is enormous. The depth of the homicide's emotional impact on her was indescribable.

We know that women of any age are twice as likely to develop post-traumatic disorder than men.

"Any questions so far?" she asked.

"No. I'm following," said Doug.

She continued.

"Psychological reactions to criminal victimizations—which she endured—can range from mild to severe. Victims such as Taylor may show a delayed onset when at least six months have passed between the traumatic event and the onset of PTD symptoms. Those symptoms usually wax and wane, coming back and then going into a remission for a time.

"I believe that when Taylor saw the hunter, she attacked him because she perceived him as a threat to her personal safety."

"Uh, excuse me. Did you say Taylor attacked a hunter? There was some kind of physical altercation?" asked Doug incredulously.

"Why, yes. I thought you knew that."

"No, I didn't. I was told some deer hunters found her in the woods and got her help."

"Well, that is true, but when Taylor saw the armed hunter, she panicked and attacked him, believing she was a potential target. Her fear of being revictimized was just as powerful as a post-victimization reaction."

"What happened to the hunter?" Doug asked, more than a bit curious.

"From what I understand, your daughter worked him over pretty good."

"What was his name? How might I speak to him?"

"There was a police report. I'm sure the police can provide you with the necessary information."

"Thank you. I'll check that out. Is the man okay?"

"Yes, I think he is. He was treated and released."

"So, back to Taylor. Seventy-five percent of homicide survivors display symptoms of PTSD as they work through the grieving process. I understand today was the first anniversary of her mother's death."

"Yes. Yes, it is."

"Victims respond to trauma and disaster differently, with some coping extremely well while others struggle. Had the hunters armed with rifles not been there, Taylor may have come to terms with whatever she needed to—to vent her emotions, to restore some form of personal control, or to prepare for what she needed to do next. I'm not sure, but things went awry with the presence of the hunter, and it clearly became a stressor, which led to her panic.

"So, with all of that said, we have given her an antidepressant and meds for anxiety. She is resting comfortably right now. In about eight hours I think she will be stabilized and doing much better.

"I suggest group therapy. I think it would prove very beneficial to her. To hear others who have experienced similar deaths of their loved ones verbalize their feelings can help heal.

"Your family has been through a lot, Mr. Conrad. You have my deepest sympathy. We will do our best to get your daughter through this."

"Thanks so much, Dr. Felderman. I have all the confidence that you can do that."

"Now, if you'll follow me, I'll take you to see Taylor."

CHAPTER 91

Doug followed Dr. Felderman into Taylor's room. Taylor was wearing a hospital gown, lying on her back sound to sleep. She looked so natural and truly at peace. The sides were up on her bed, but with little effort, Doug was able to extend his upper torso over the rail and kiss Taylor on the forehead. He took her hand and held it as he studied her face.

"I'm going back to work. Feel free to stay as long as you wish, Mr. Conrad. I'm sure she'll be happy to see you when she wakes up."

Doug pulled a chair up closer to her bed. For the next thirty minutes, he held Taylor's limp hand and prayed for her. How does anyone recover from a year like they had had? His mother used to say, "No matter how many cloudy days we may have, we know the sun will eventually shine again, so like the weather, son, we just wait patiently for the sun."

A staff member quietly walked into the room and gently tapped Doug on the shoulder.

"Mr. Conrad, there's a Lieutenant Sanders down in the main lobby to see you."

"Oh, good. Thank you. I'd like to talk to him too."

Doug made his way to the lobby and walked over to the only man in a police uniform. Lieutenant Sanders was watching for him too. Both men introduced himself at the same time.

"Mr. Conrad, your daughter's car is sitting in the parking lot of our police station." He then handed Doug a shopping bag.

"Here. This is for you."

Doug looked in the bag. It was Taylor's purse.

"Her car keys are in her purse along with her wallet and whatever she had. Her car will be safe in our lot, so you don't have to be in a hurry to get it out of there."

Just then, Paul Conrad walked in to the hospital and saw his father talking to a police officer. He walked right over to them.

"Hi, Dad."

"Hi. This is Paul, my son, and this is Lieutenant Sanders, Paul."

Both men exchanged handshakes.

"Perhaps we could all go to the cafeteria for a Coke. As a courtesy to you, I'd like to talk to you and fill you in on what we know about this morning."

"Yes. Please do."

Once they sat down in a corner booth, Lieutenant Sanders began to share the events that led up to Taylor being in the hospital.

"Here's what we know. A young man named Chase Manning was in the woods to deer hunt. He's twenty-five years old and his buddy, Greg Marshall, dropped him off at the deer site and then he drove to a nearby location to set up his deer blind. It was around five-ish. Chase said he saw vehicle lights come down the path while he was sitting in—well, Brady Randolph's deer blind—and then he saw a dim light moving around the shed. The light went off, and then he heard someone or something sprinting down the path toward him. At first he wasn't sure if it was a deer that was scared up or a human.

"Chase is a well-trained hunter. You don't shoot unless you can see the target and, besides, it wasn't daylight yet, so he couldn't shoot. Then he realized the footsteps were that of a female. Apparently your daughter lay on the ground and was talking out loud to her mother. Chase thought he knew who she was. He could tell she was very distraught. He decided to come down out of the tree to talk to her. As he was leaning his rifle against the tree, she turned her flashlight on, saw his rifle, and believed her life was in danger. She began to attack him. Now Chase is a big guy. He's also a gentleman. He doesn't hit women, but she was pretty much in attack mode. He tried to fend her off and identify himself to her, but it was as though she didn't even hear him.

"Chase knew by then who she was—everyone around here remembers this case. So he calls his hunting buddy on his cell phone and tells him to call the police and an ambulance and tells his buddy to come and help him.

"She even attacked us when we arrived," said Sanders.

"Geez!" said Paul in disbelief.

"She was taken to the hospital. Clearly she was having a panic attack and needed help." He paused for a moment as though in thought. "This is a good hospital, Mr. Conrad. She'll get good care here. Don't you worry."

"Thank you. I'm sure it is. So how do I find this Chase Manning? Is he okay?" asked Doug.

"Well, he incurred some injuries that required medical attention. He had deep bites on both hands and some pretty bad facial scratches. She also head butted him and busted his nose pretty good, not to mention kicking him. He's bruised pretty badly and may be singing soprano in the church choir for life, according to him."

"Oh, man!" said Paul. "Sounds like this guy needed to take wrestling in school."

"Actually, the guy is six-feet-four and a big bruiser. He's a former marine with combat training under his belt, so I'd say he used a lot of restraint with Taylor."

Both Doug and Paul seemed a little surprised with that information.

"Oh, and there's one more thing you might find interesting about this guy," said Sanders.

"What's that?" asked Paul.

"When he was a senior in high school, his mother was murdered while working in their family-owned jewelry store. Right in the heart of downtown, in the middle of the day. So I think he was trying to show compassion for this young lady once he realized who she was."

Paul looked over at his dad. Both men were speechless.

"May we meet him, Lieutenant Sanders?" asked Doug.

"How about if I give him your cell phone number, and if he would like to talk to you or meet you, he can initiate it?"

"That would be fine," said Doug. He handed Lieutenant Sanders one of his business cards.

CHAPTER 92

Doug and Paul stayed at a Sleep Inn overnight. After breakfast, they headed for the hospital. Paul would visit Taylor one more time and then he needed to head back to OSU. It was important that he be there for Taylor and for his dad. It was a time when they all needed to be together.

On the way to the hospital, Paul turned to his dad in the car.

"Do you suppose we could drive to the scene where Mom died, Dad?"

"Do you really want to go there, Paul?"

"Well, since we're already here . . . we know about the shed and the path to nowhere, I guess I'm just curious. There was something about it that drew Taylor to it. Maybe we will feel closer to Mom."

"What if you have an emotional setback like Taylor?"

"Aren't you at least curious about it, Dad?"

"Yes, but I wasn't sure I could ever bring myself to actually go there."

"We don't have to go, Dad."

Doug figured eventually Paul would choose to go there too, so rather than go alone, it would be better if he was there with him. Doug turned the car in the direction of the highway that would lead outside of Parkersburg. He knew from the trial exactly how to find this place. He saw the maps displayed for the jury and had memorized it.

This might be the worst mistake he had ever made. He remembered vaguely reading a novel once called *The Shed*. It was about returning to a place where a child had been murdered and finding healing. It's like

Dr. Felderman said, "Victims respond to trauma and disaster differently. Some cope extremely well while others struggle."

Twenty minutes later, Doug found the dirt road that led down to the shed. Both men sat in the car just staring at it. Neither said anything.

After quite some time, they got out of the car and surveyed the area with their eyes. Descriptions and things that were said in trial were coming back. Right before them was the path. Both men stood there looking down it. Thinking, picturing, wondering.

Not a word was said between them, but both men began walking down the path. These were Cynthia's last steps while on earth. The very last thing she would see. When they reached the end of the path, they felt a sense of desolation. Doug put his arm around his son, and Paul put his arm around his dad's waist. They stood there with tears streaming down their faces.

Doug turned and totally embraced his son. It was all pretty overwhelming. Both cried. It had been a cloudy day, and just then the sun broke through the trees and lit the path. It was so bright. They could feel the warmth of the sun on their back. It was, well, comforting.

And then Doug remembered his mother's words, which he spoke out loud, "No matter how many cloudy days we may have in our lives, the sun will eventually shine again."

"Maybe mom's trying to tell us that today, Dad."

"I think maybe she is, son."

Quietly they walked back to the car in silence and never looked back.

CHAPTER 93

P aul and Doug were sitting by Taylor's bedside once again. She had awakened and looked alert although you could tell she was under the influence of a drug that had made her overly relaxed and nonchalant.

Doug's cell phone rang. Doug answered it.

"Mr. Conrad. I'm Chase Manning. I'm the deer—"

"Yes, I know who you are. Thank you for calling. My son and I are indebted to you."

"Well, I'm in the lobby of the hospital, and I was hoping to meet you and check on your daughter, but without your permission, I can't get past Mrs. Johnston here at the desk."

"I'll be right down, Chase."

Doug went to the information desk and saw a young man standing there who fit Lieutenant Sanders's description of Chase. He was at least six feet four and built like a marine. Doug noticed how polished his shoes were. He was wearing nice trousers, a navy blue V-necked sweater with a crisp white shirt underneath it, and had a blue-and-gold striped tie on. He had thick, short-cropped dark brown hair and was clean shaven.

Mrs. Johnston saw the men shake hands and then both turned and headed for the elevator. They talked all the way up to the fourth floor.

Dr. Felderman had already heard that Chase Manning had come to visit Taylor and thought it best she be in the room to monitor their second introduction to one another.

Doug introduced Chase to Paul. They shook hands, and Doug could see Paul observing every little detail about this guy. He was a sight to behold. He had terrible scratches down both cheeks. His one eye was swollen and actually pretty bruised. But when Paul shook his hands, he noticed the deep bite mark on top. It looked terrible and painful. Then he saw his other hand, which looked even worse.

Doug walked Chase over to the left side of Taylor's bed and introduced him to her. It was obvious that she wasn't cognizant as to who he was and why she was meeting him. She did notice that he was dressed nicely and was very good looking, but the scratches down his cheeks and his swollen eye were obvious too. When she went to shake his hand after the introduction, she saw the wounds on both his hands.

"So what happened to you?" Taylor asked rather bluntly.

Chase just stood there for a minute, a bit surprised by her blunt comment. It seemed she didn't remember anything from yesterday morning. She had blocked it all out.

"Well, let's just say I was on a safari that turned a little wild once I ran in to a lioness."

"Really? Were you in Africa?" Taylor asked innocently.

"No. Actually I was right here in Parkersburg."

"I had no idea Parkersburg had lions."

"Nor did I," said Chase playing along.

"Wow! Then you're quite lucky to be alive!" Taylor said with astonishment.

"Yes. I guess I am."

Everyone in the room couldn't help but laugh.

Chase turned around to Dr. Felderman because he didn't know what he should do or say next. Dr. Felderman stepped forward and very succinctly explained to Taylor who Chase was and why he was here. She didn't want this to be a charade. She needed Taylor to face the truth and try to remember her eventful morning.

"So you're saying I did all of that to him?" she asked, not believing any of it.

"Actually, yes," said Chase stepping in to the conversation once again. "I understood what was happening to you. At least I think I did."

"You can't possibly know unless your mother was murdered," Taylor said.

"Well, then, I can know."

"You mean your mother was murdered too? In those woods?" asked Taylor.

"No. My family owns a high-end jewelry store in downtown Parkersburg. I was a senior in high school when my mom was murdered. My dad had just left the store to deposit a large sum of money to the bank, leaving my mom to work in the store alone. He would be back in ten or fifteen minutes. While Dad was gone, an armed robber came in and demanded my mom open the glass display of diamond rings and a cash register. She was so nervous she couldn't find the right key to the display or get the cash register open fast enough, so he shot and killed her. When my dad returned to the store, he found my mom on the floor behind the counter. Dead. We had a camera in our store, but none on the outside like we have today. My dad felt guilty for leaving my mother alone in the store that day.

"After high school, my dad felt it best for me to join the marines and step away from the family store and our surroundings. The original plan was to go to college and study business while continuing to help out in our family store, but after Mom's murder, he wanted me to have more time to recover. Retrospectively, I think that was the right decision. I spent three years in the marines, and with the help of the GI Bill, I just graduated with a four-year business degree.

"Oh, and by the way, I brought you something." He handed her a small box beautifully wrapped with a lovely bow on it.

"What is it?" Taylor asked.

"Open it up and see," said Chase.

Taylor opened it up. It was a delicate gold chain necklace with a gold pineapple pendant on it. It was lovely, and it was obvious it was very expensive. The chain sparkled.

Chase helped her put it on.

"The pineapple is a symbol of friendship, Taylor. If you promise not to bite, kick, or sucker punch me anymore, I'm sure we could be good friends."

"I sucker punched you?" Taylor asked.

"Yep! A big guy like me. I didn't see it coming."

Taylor had to laugh even though she could hardly believe she had done that.

"I'm so sorry. I don't even remember doing it. I don't even remember you, actually," she confessed.

"After all of that, you give me a necklace?"

"Yeah. I'd rather be your friend than your foe. Can we make a deal on that?"

"We sure can. Chase, I don't know what to say except thank you. This is so sweet."

Paul told his sister good-bye and slipped out of the room. Doug followed behind him to say good-bye.

"Geez, Dad! Did you see how Taylor was looking at this guy? She may be a little looped right now, but I have a feeling this guy just walked into her life for a reason."

Doug laughed. "I was thinking the same thing, Paul. Like Pastor Jim Pascoe keeps saying, 'God works in mysterious ways!'"

CHAPTER 94

The next day Doug met with Dr. Felderman. Taylor seemed to be doing much better. She had found a very nice friend in Chase Manning and had been actively participating in group therapy. Dr. Felderman felt Taylor needed to stay a few days longer before she would release her with the recommendation that she participate in more counseling and group therapy once she returns to Akron. Taylor seemed to be satisfied with that.

Doug needed to return to work and would commute to Parkersburg for the next several days. Taylor told him it wasn't necessary. Chase had promised to visit her once a day and even volunteered to drive her and her car back to Akron, with Greg following behind them in his car. While Doug wasn't crazy about the idea, he saw that Taylor was quite smitten by this guy and was excited about the plan. Because of Taylor's age, he would eventually have to let go. He was still carrying the father protective gene inside him, and perhaps even more now than he had two days ago. He had met Chase, liked him, and had a good impression of him. Unknown to anyone else, however, he did a little detective research on him and learned he was as squeaky clean as he appeared.

He noted that Taylor was proudly wearing the necklace Chase had given to her, and after many months, Doug was finally looking in the face of a happy young daughter. That was worth plenty to him. He gave her a big hug and kiss and reminded her that he was only a call away.

While on the highway heading for Akron, Doug was eager to get back to his office and back to routine.

CHAPTER 95

As he pulled in to his office parking lot, Doug saw Barnabus walking in to the office. Donna's car wasn't there. He hoped Stella was doing all right.

Barnabus and Jean were standing in the doorway of Mitch's office. As soon as they saw Doug, they were curious to hear an update on Taylor. It was like one big, happy family.

They decided to march into the larger conference room and hold a meeting. Really, it was more of an update on everyone's situation than a discussion of their cases. Before they grabbed their coffee mugs, Donna walked in. Now the family circle was complete.

"How's your mom?" asked Doug.

"I think the doctor's going to discharge her this afternoon. She's doing fine and ready to come home."

Barnabus was quite surprised to hear about the church takeover and about Donna's mother being shot. He hadn't listened to the news for over a week.

"So what happened in your meeting with Bates?" Doug asked.

Donna smiled sheepishly.

"Well, for the first ten minutes, he chewed me out—up one side and down the other for disobeying him and going into the church.

"Then he praised the beauty of my properly functioning spy pen. He found the frequency I was on with it, and I was able to give him a very detailed report of everything that happened inside the church once I got inside and what actually provoked Eddie Flatt to push him over the edge. Then he wasn't so angry with me. We knew if only Olivia Rainey had

had four Restoril tablets in her pocket that day instead of just two, no one would have even gotten hurt, and it would have ended peaceably."

"So how did these goonies pick your church?" asked Jean.

"It turns out Waneda Robinson had been an earlier target for one of their scams, but she didn't take the bait. Not to be outwitted by an 'old lady,' they followed her for days to learn her routine. Grocery store, hair salon, and church. So they decided to go to the church and steal the ladies' purses—grabbing quick money, charge cards, gift cards, whatever.

"Commander Bates just told me this morning that Eddie Flatt finally confessed to several murders. Bobby thought they had just stolen money from all of these old people. He didn't know that during step 2 of their scams when Eddie would drop by to collect the money that he would kill them if he sensed the elderly women were getting suspicious and could identify them. He said Bobby would never have had the stomach to do it but that it had to be done in order for them to succeed and get ahead.

"We now know Waneda had a guardian angel sitting on her shoulder or she very well might have been among the dead. Her testimony will be important to show how these guys worked the system. They've already taken a deposition from her."

"So how is Taylor, and what actually happened, Doug?" asked Mitch who had always had a special interest in Doug's kids.

Everyone listened with sympathetic hearts but seemed happy to hear about Chase Manning and what a nice guy he was. It sounded like he had come to her rescue.

Barnabus thanked everyone for their kindness to him while he was out for his grandmother's final days and then the funeral.

"I am anxious to get back to work," Barnabus remarked sincerely.

Mitch and Jean then discussed where they were on two of his cases but that they hadn't made any progress yet with the young teenager.

"Good. I wanted to work on that case myself. How about I take you all out to lunch today?" asked Barnabus.

"That's not necessary. We were just doing our job."

"I know, but I'd really like to," he insisted.

"Well, in that case, I've been hankering for some of Red Lobster's succulent lobster," said Mitch, laughing.

"Me too," said Jean and Doug simultaneously.

"Sounds good to me," said Donna, smiling.

"No problem," said Barnabus, and he meant it.

For some reason, it felt good to be back at work and be a part of Conrad Confidential. He enjoyed the camaraderie and felt the love. As he looked around the table at his cohorts, he saw Mitch who, with his wife, nearly laid down their lives protecting Doug's children when Quinton Reed broke into their home. And now he hears how Donna's mother pushed her in order to protect her from getting shot and took the bullet instead. These were all quality people who put such value on life, even at the cost of sacrificing their own. He realized how truly wise his grandmother was, and he was determined to live up to her expectations of him. Life was good!

AUTHOR'S BIOGRAPHY

Linda Lonsdorf, born in Akron, Ohio, is a retired high school speech and English instructor. She resides in Green, Ohio and Florida with her husband, Dr. W. Kevin Lonsdorf. Her lifelong passion for reading as well as her love for suspense and drama led her to write *Family Threat*, *Evil Injustice*, and now *A Deadly Ruse*.

CPSIA information can be obtained at www.ICGtesting.com
Printed in the USA
BVOW082023050313

314794BV00002B/4/P